HELLO

Aiko Ikegami

Creston Books

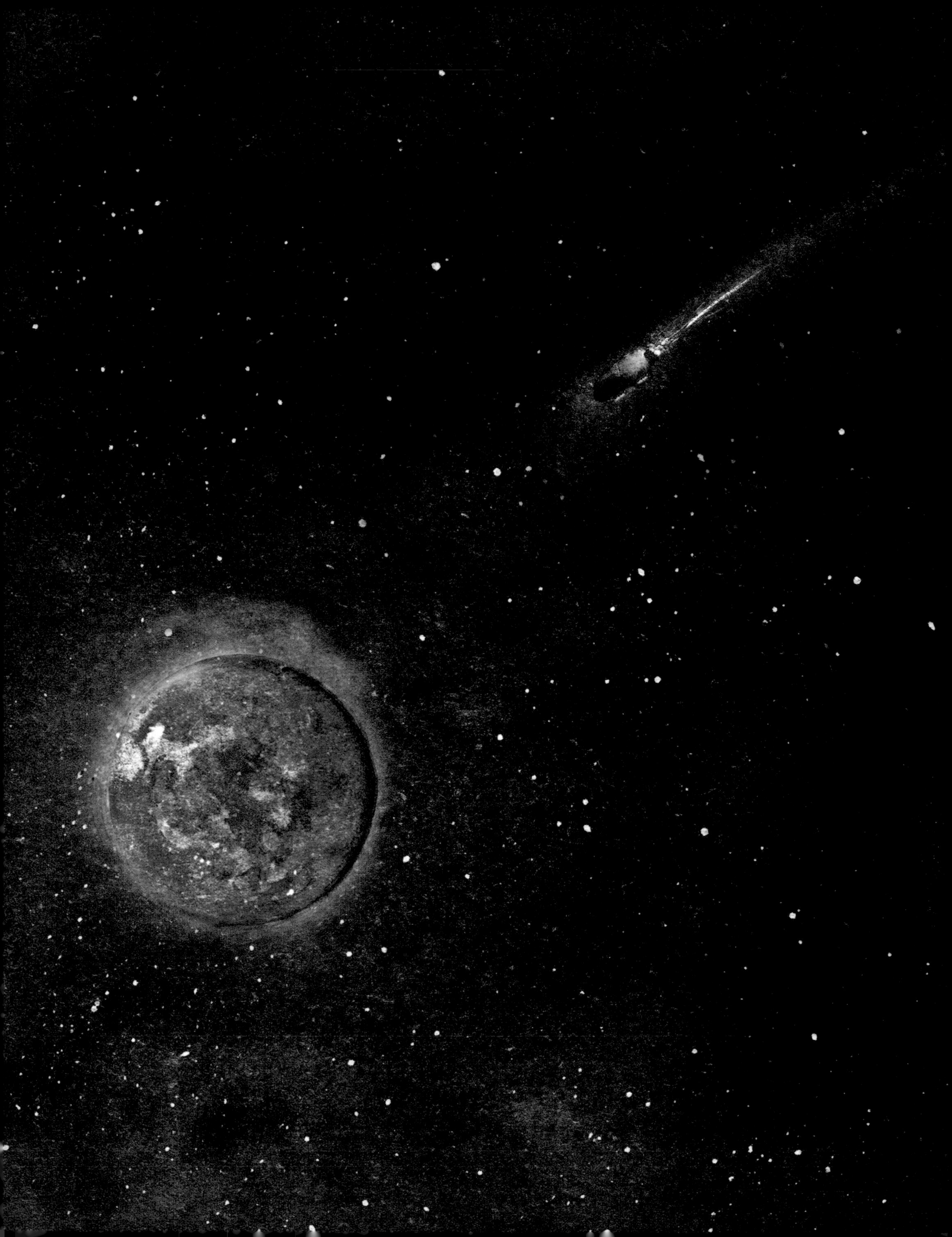

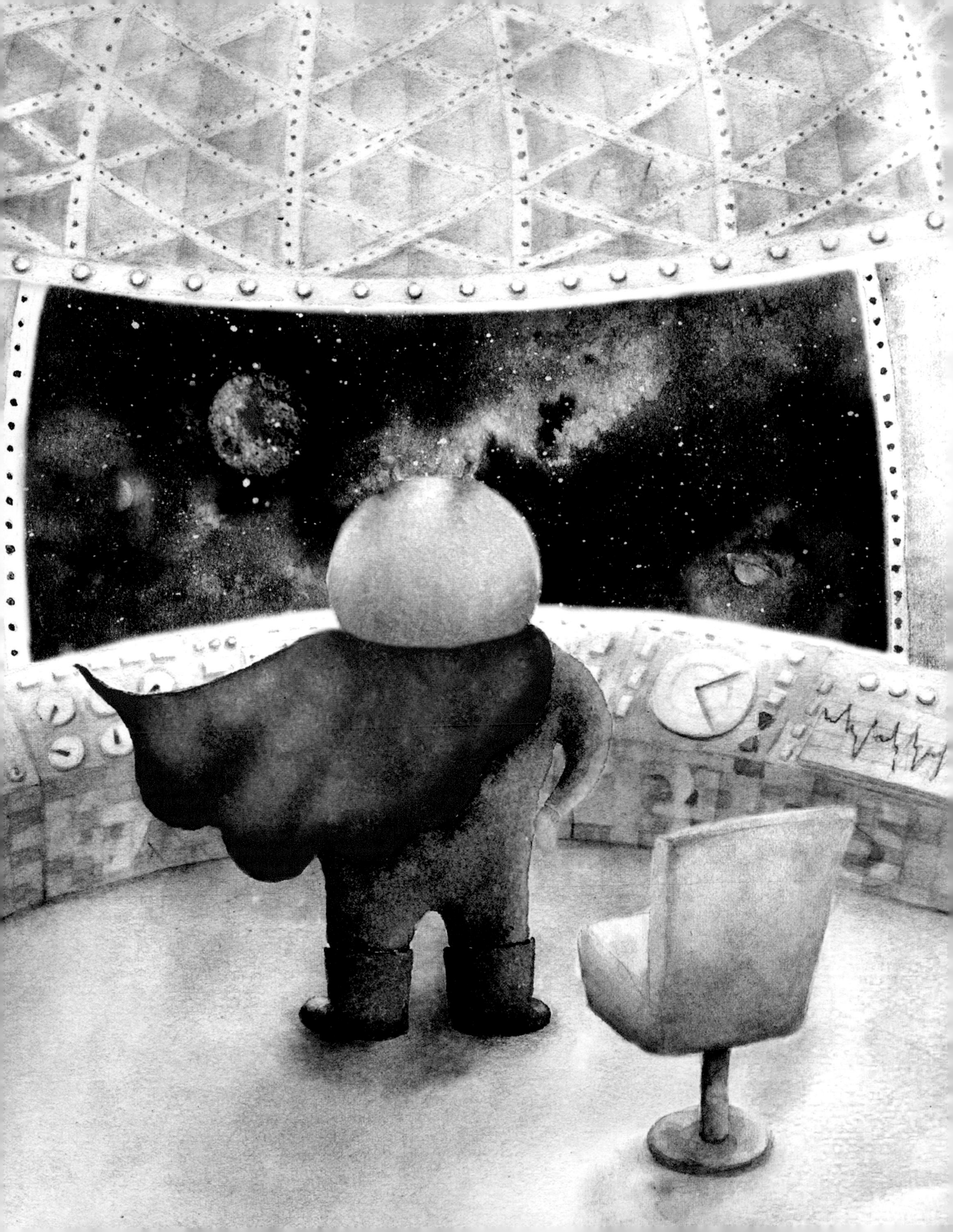

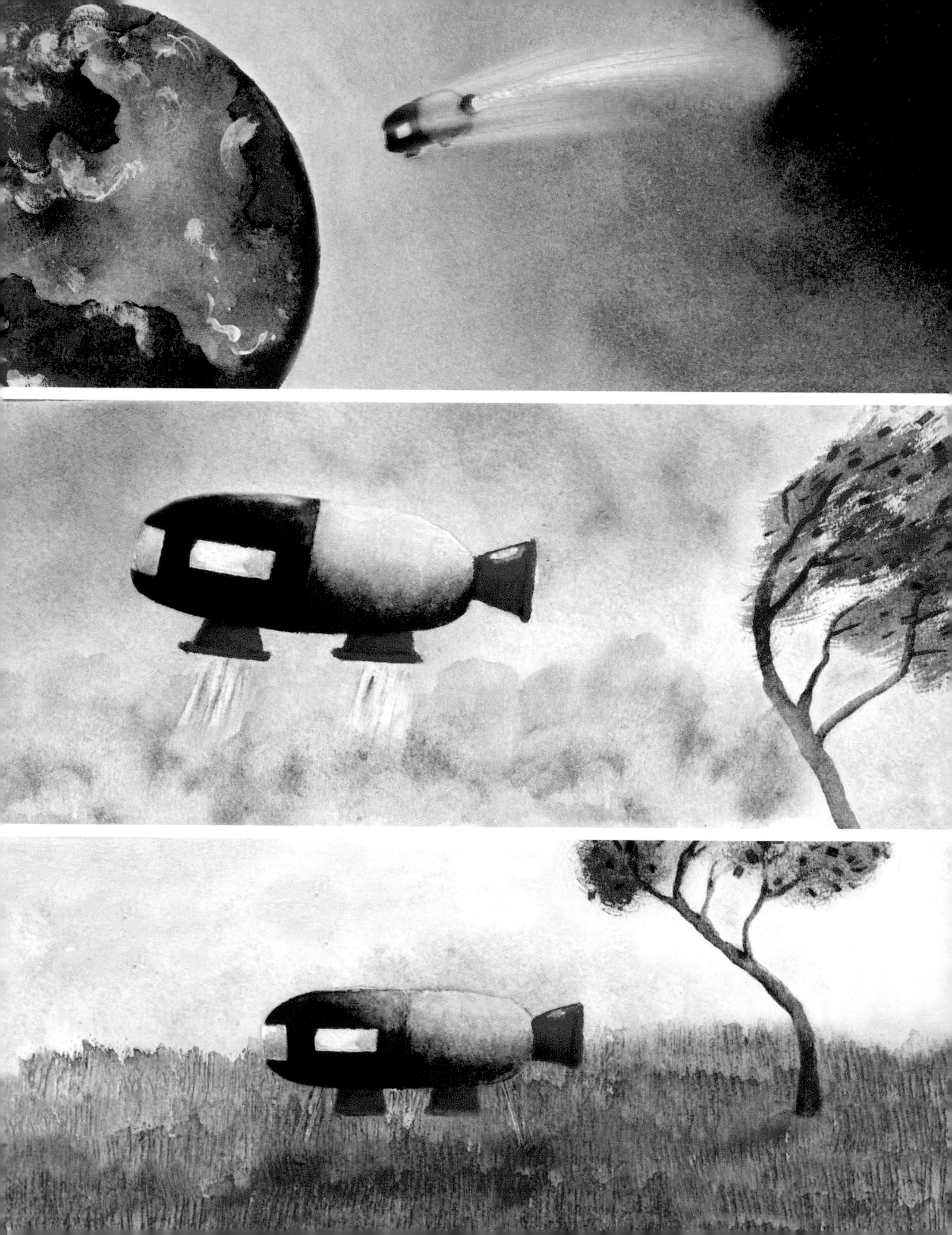

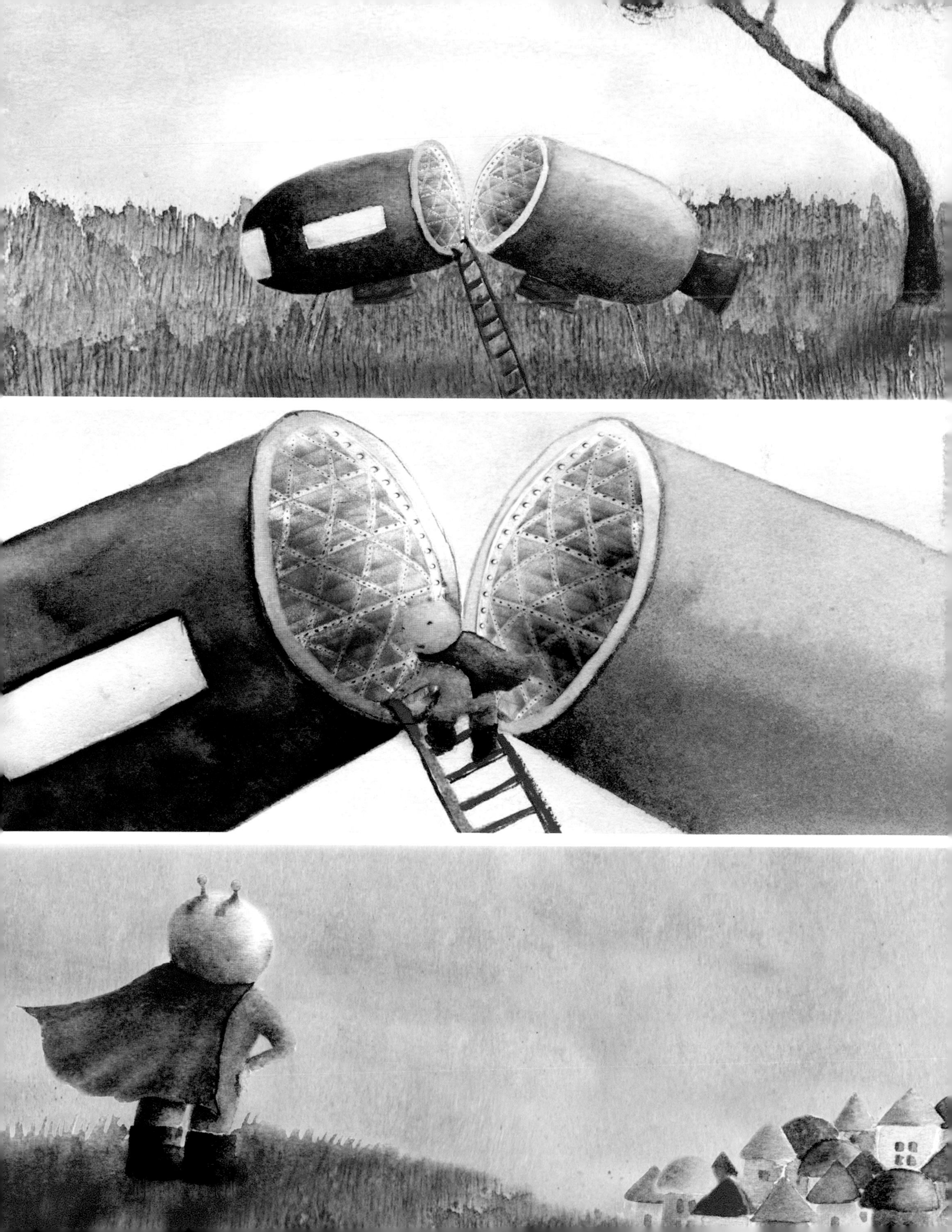

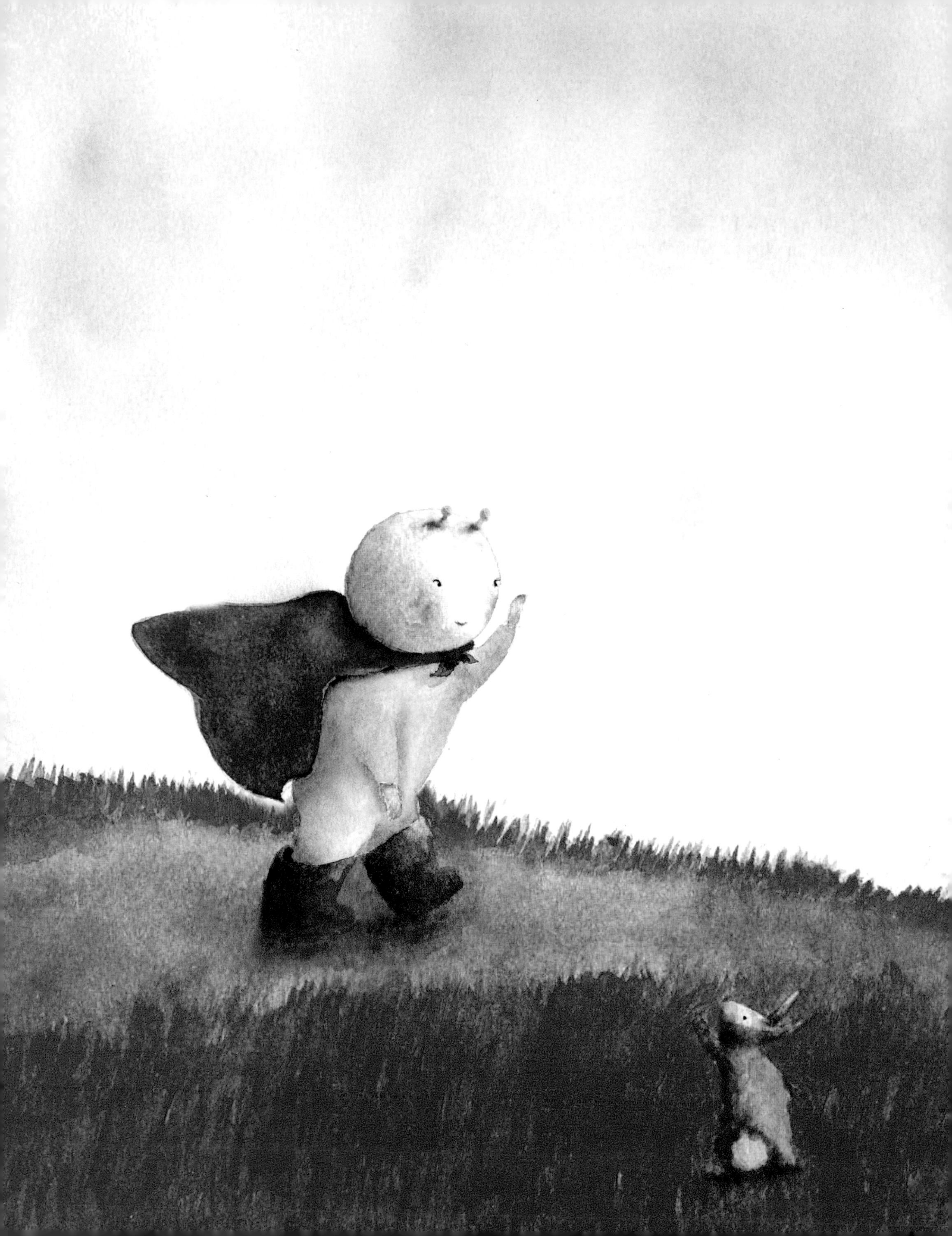

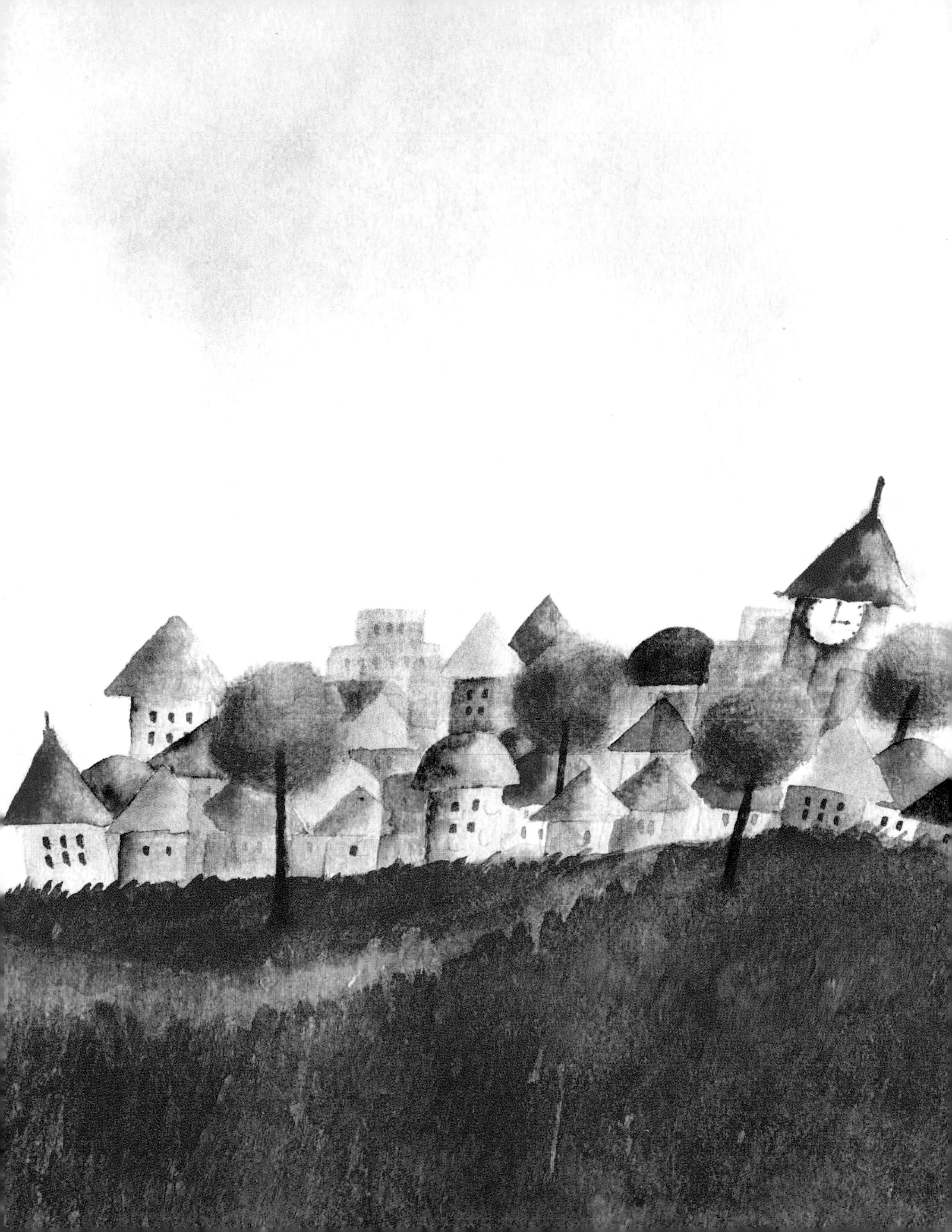

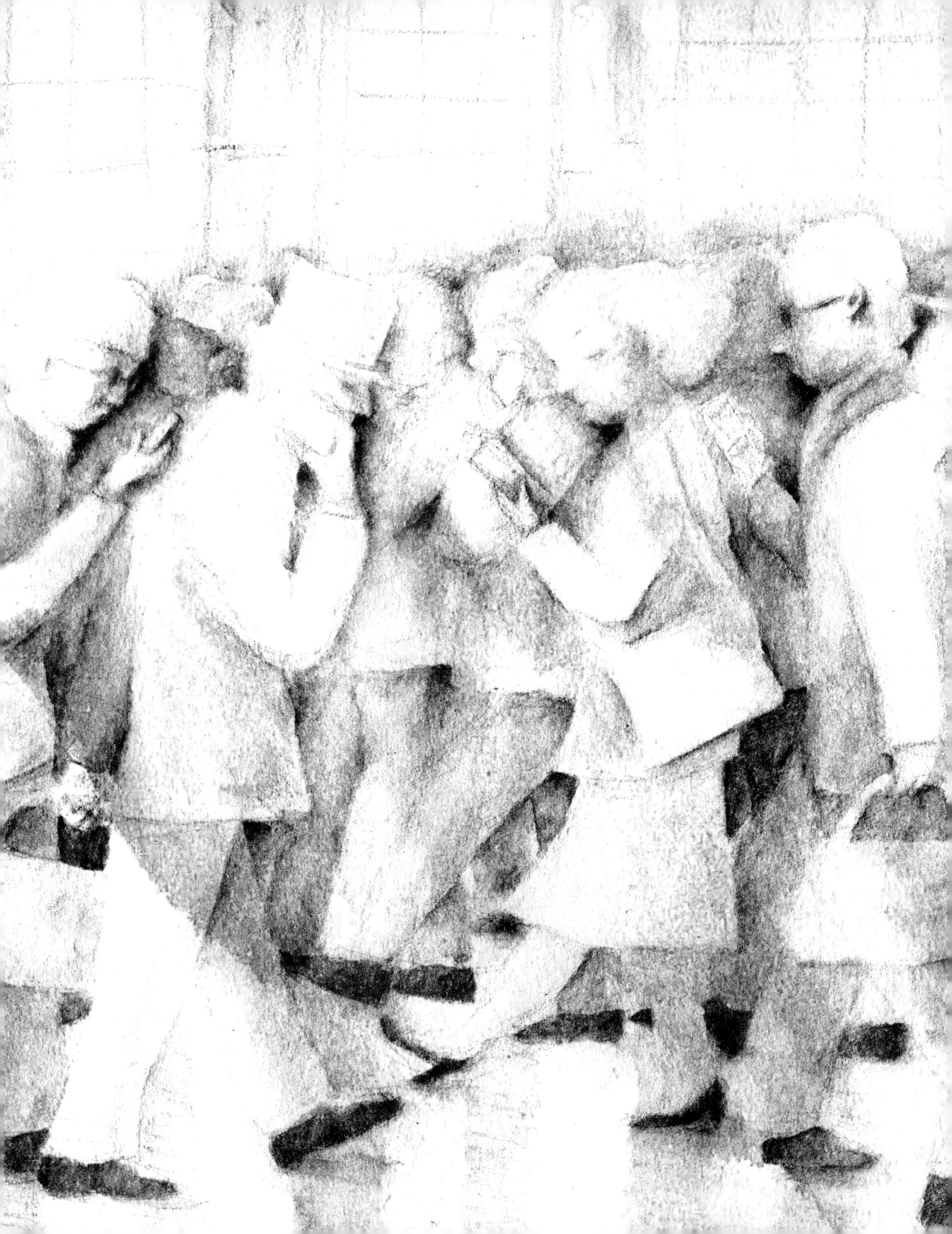

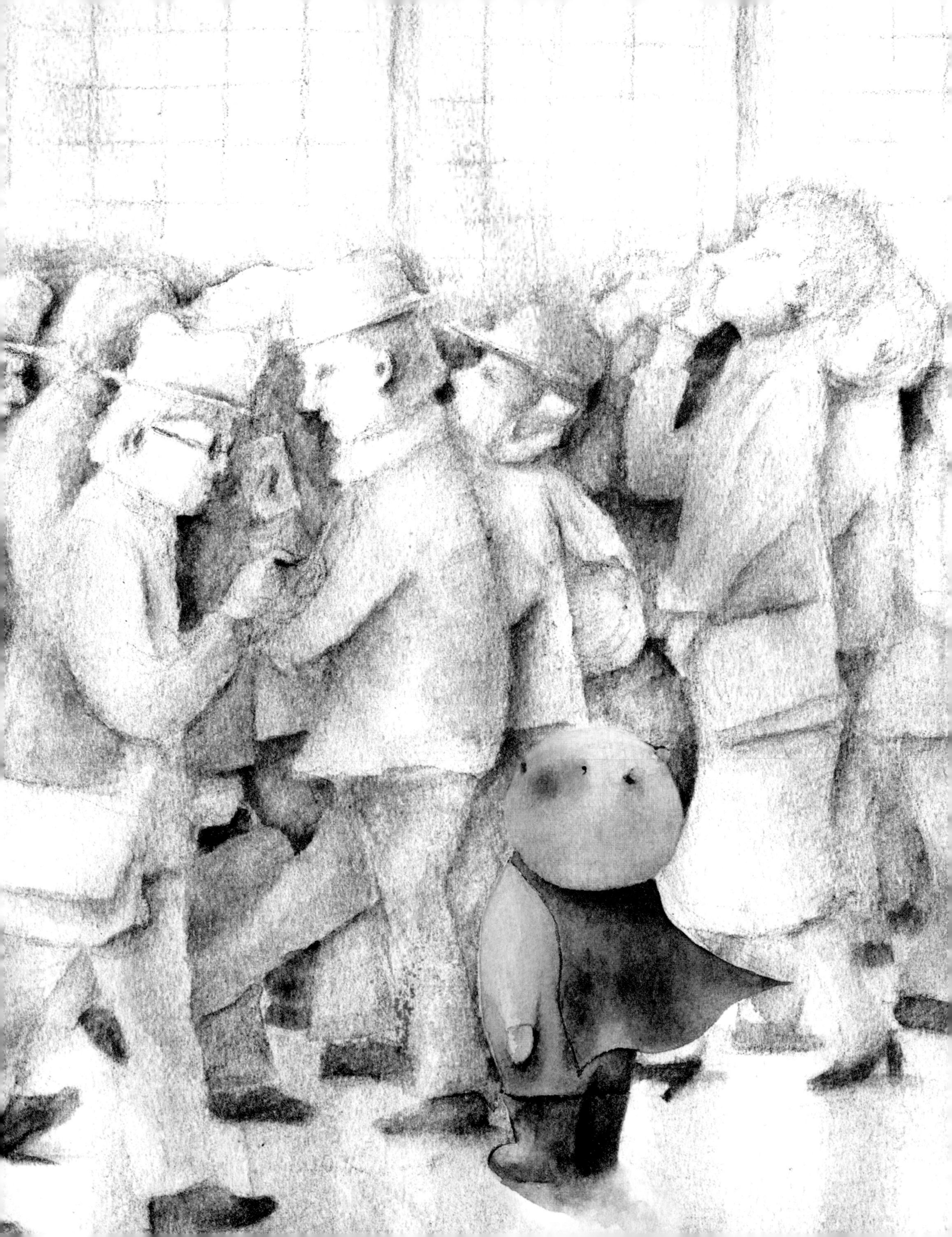

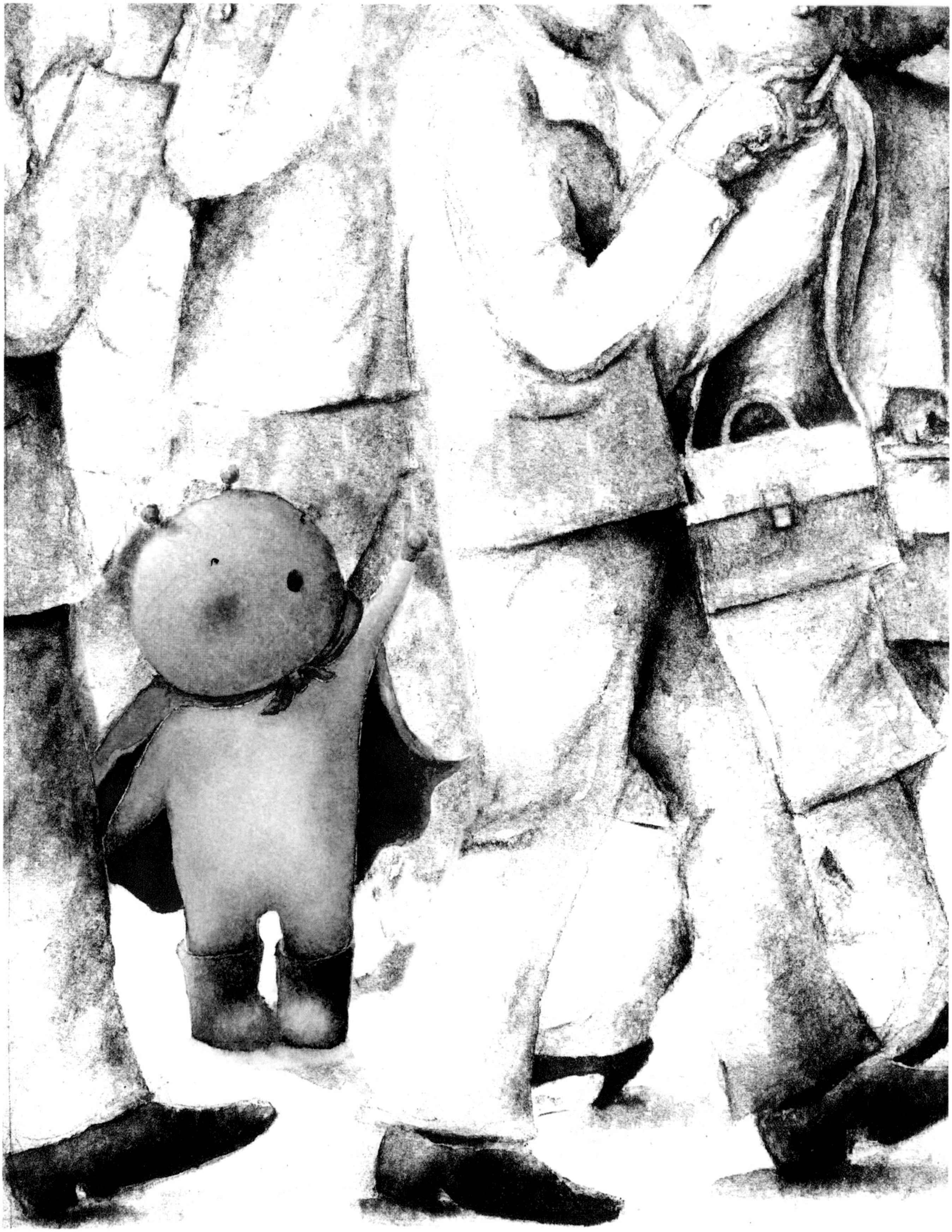

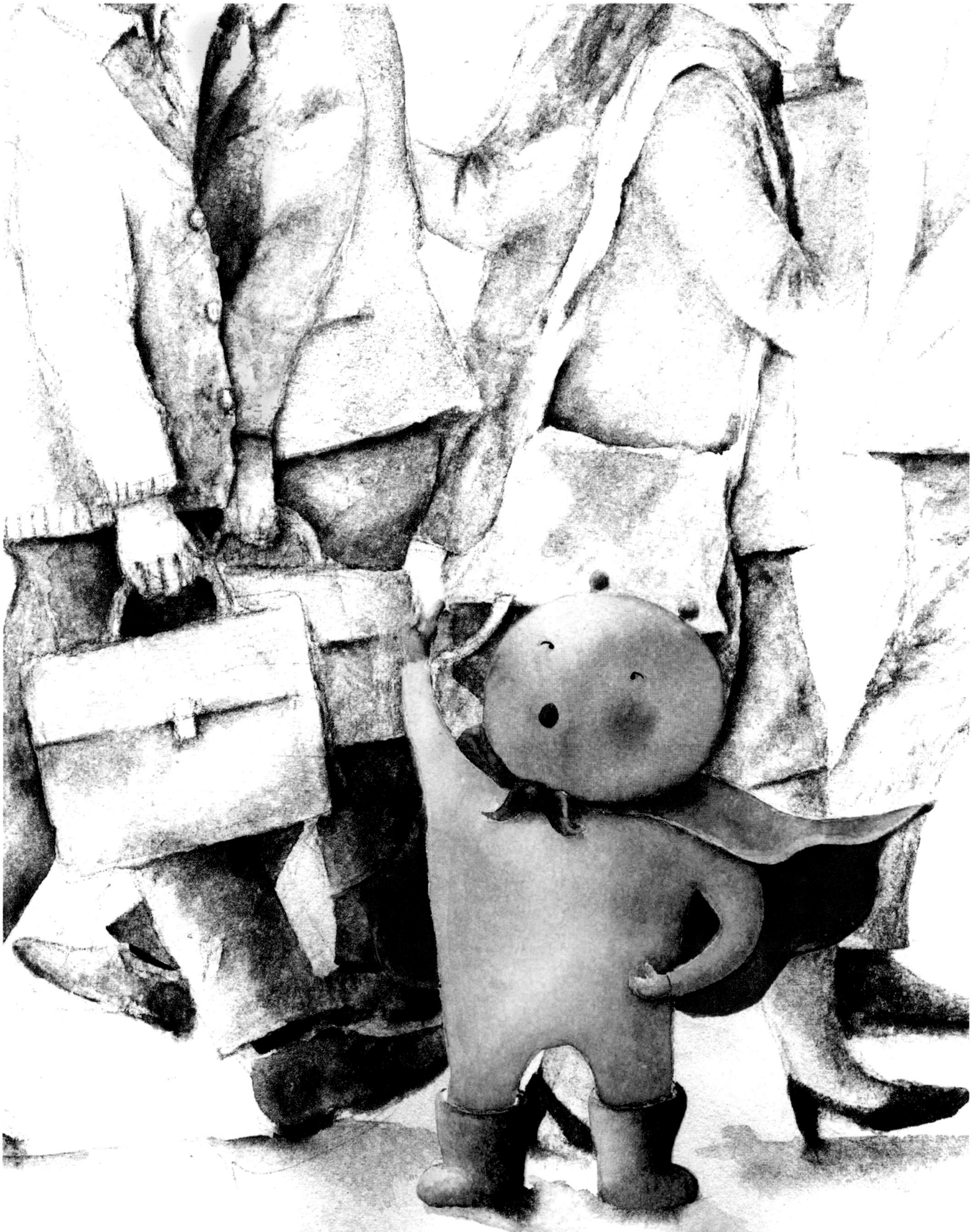

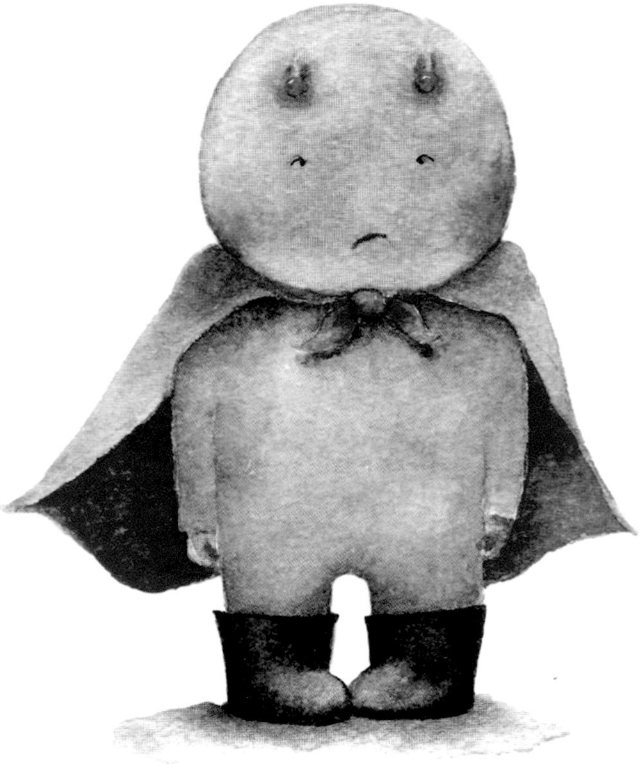

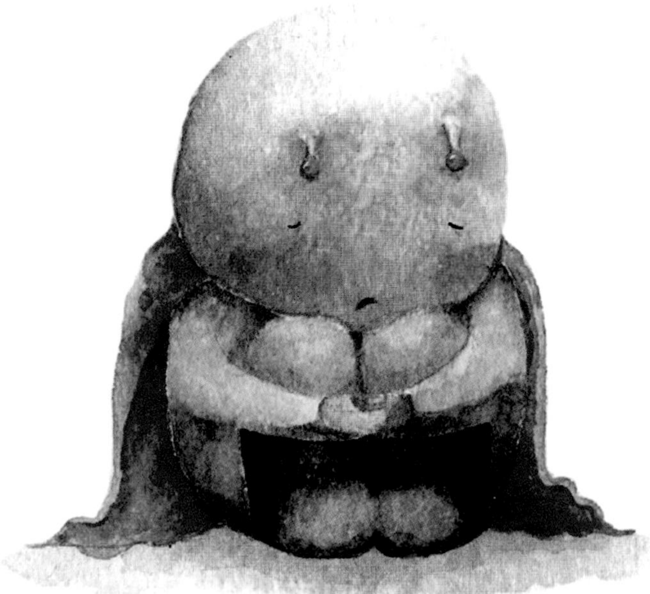

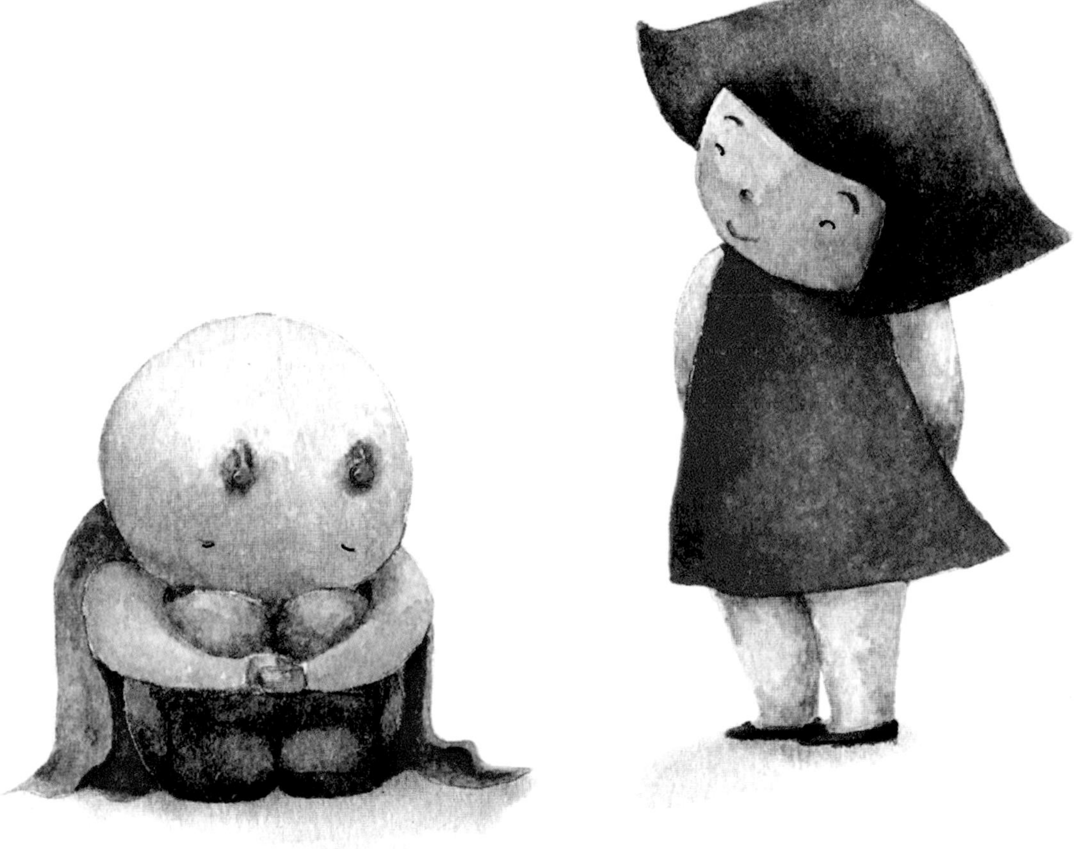

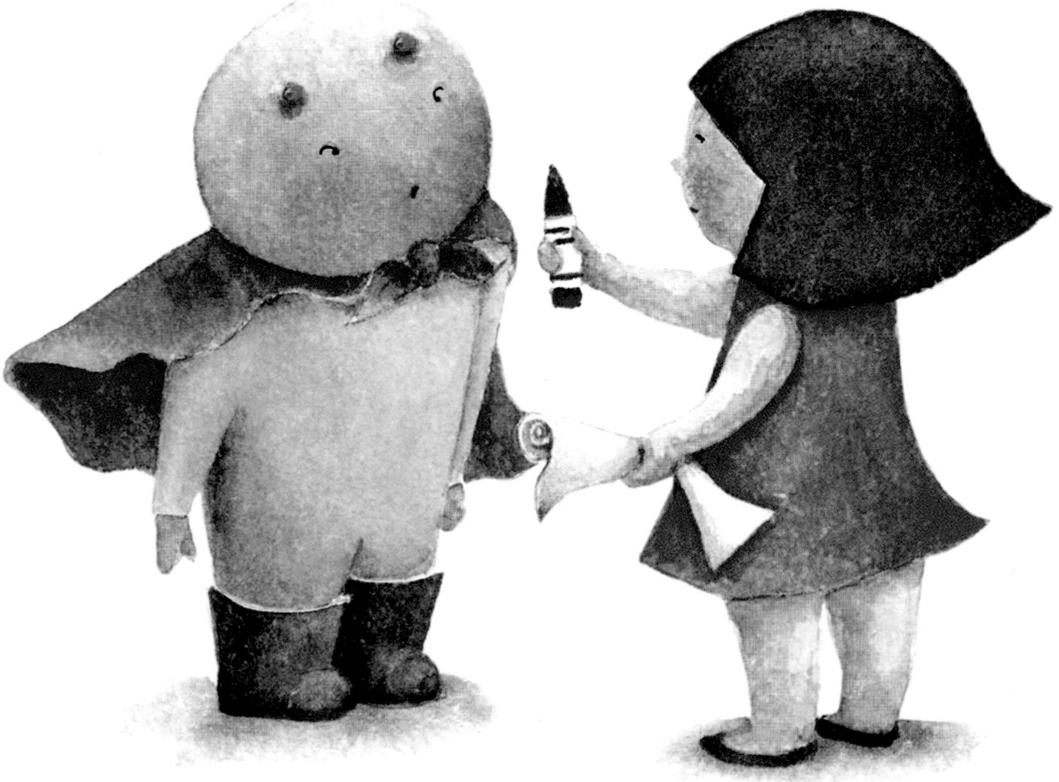

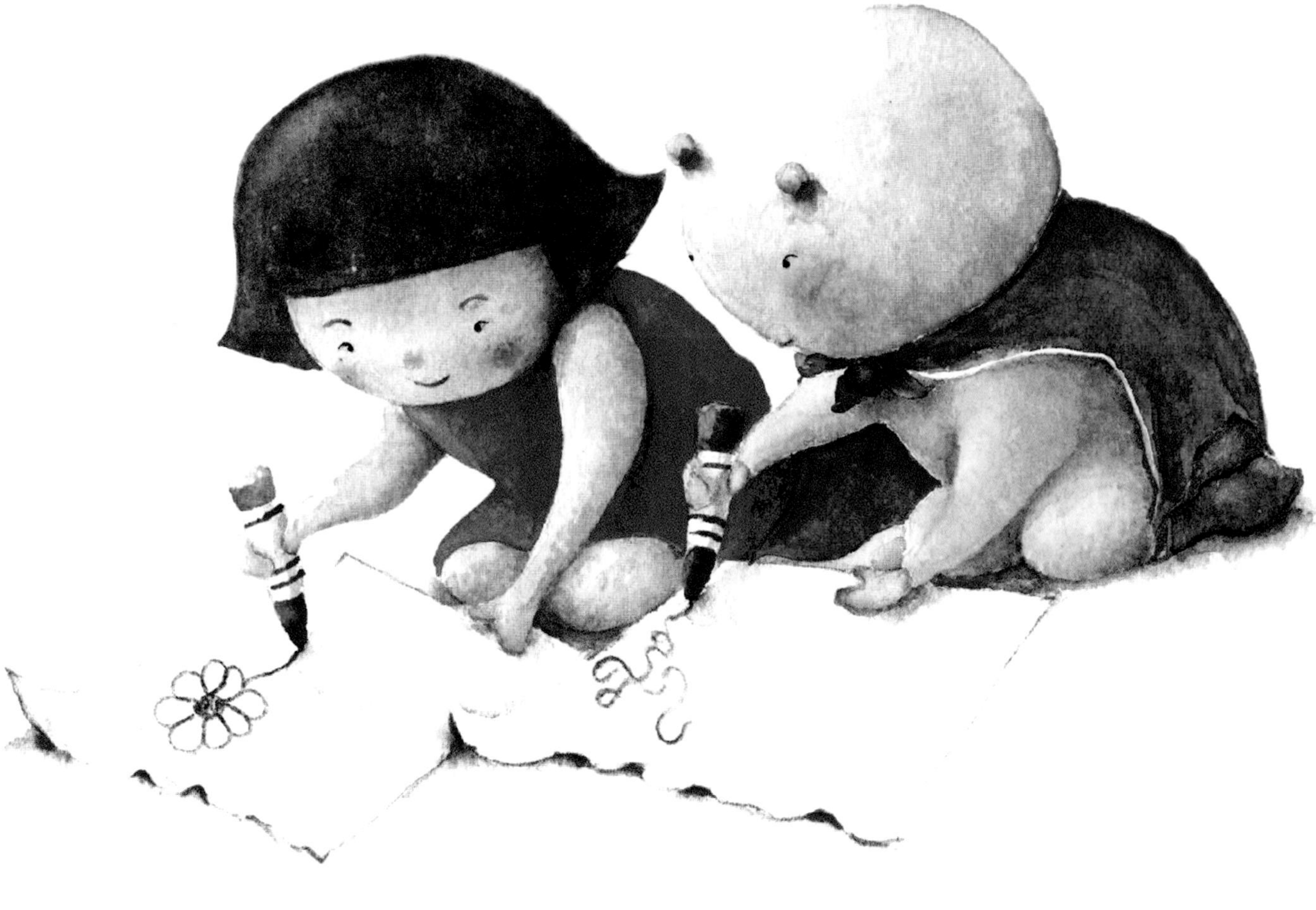

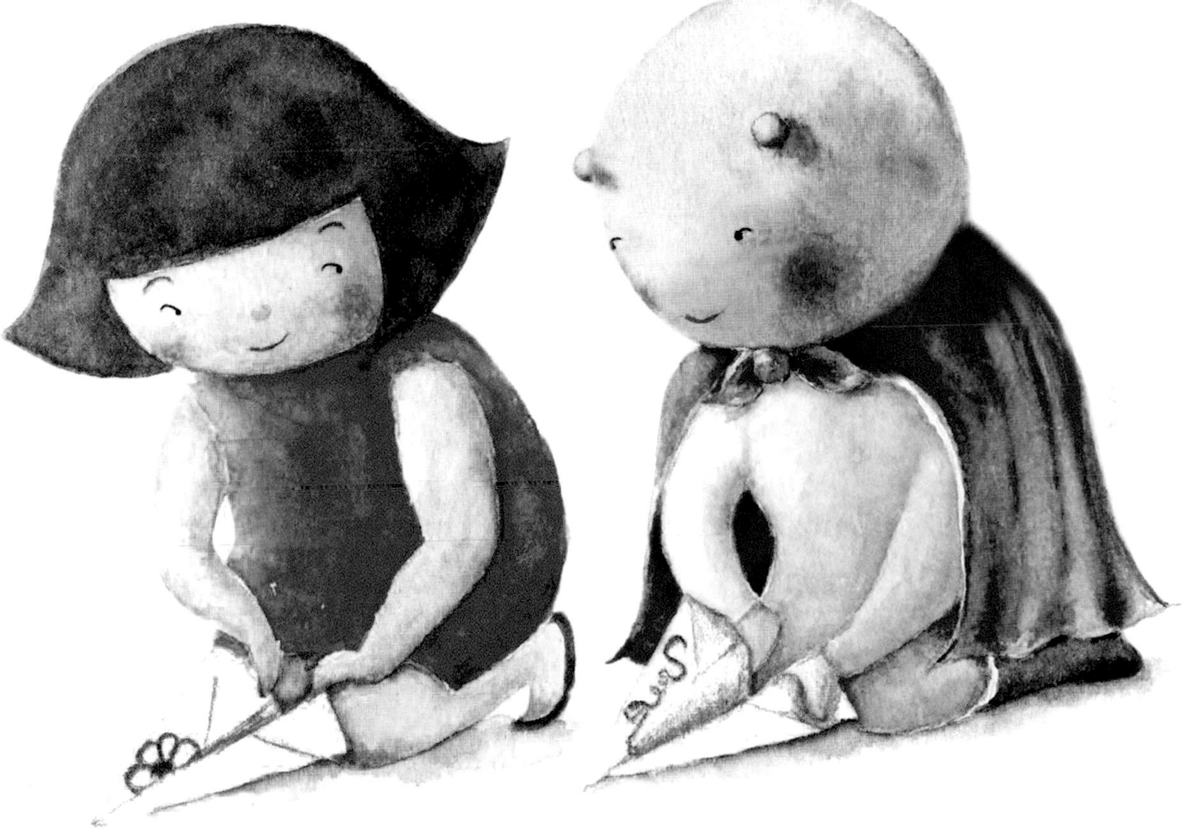

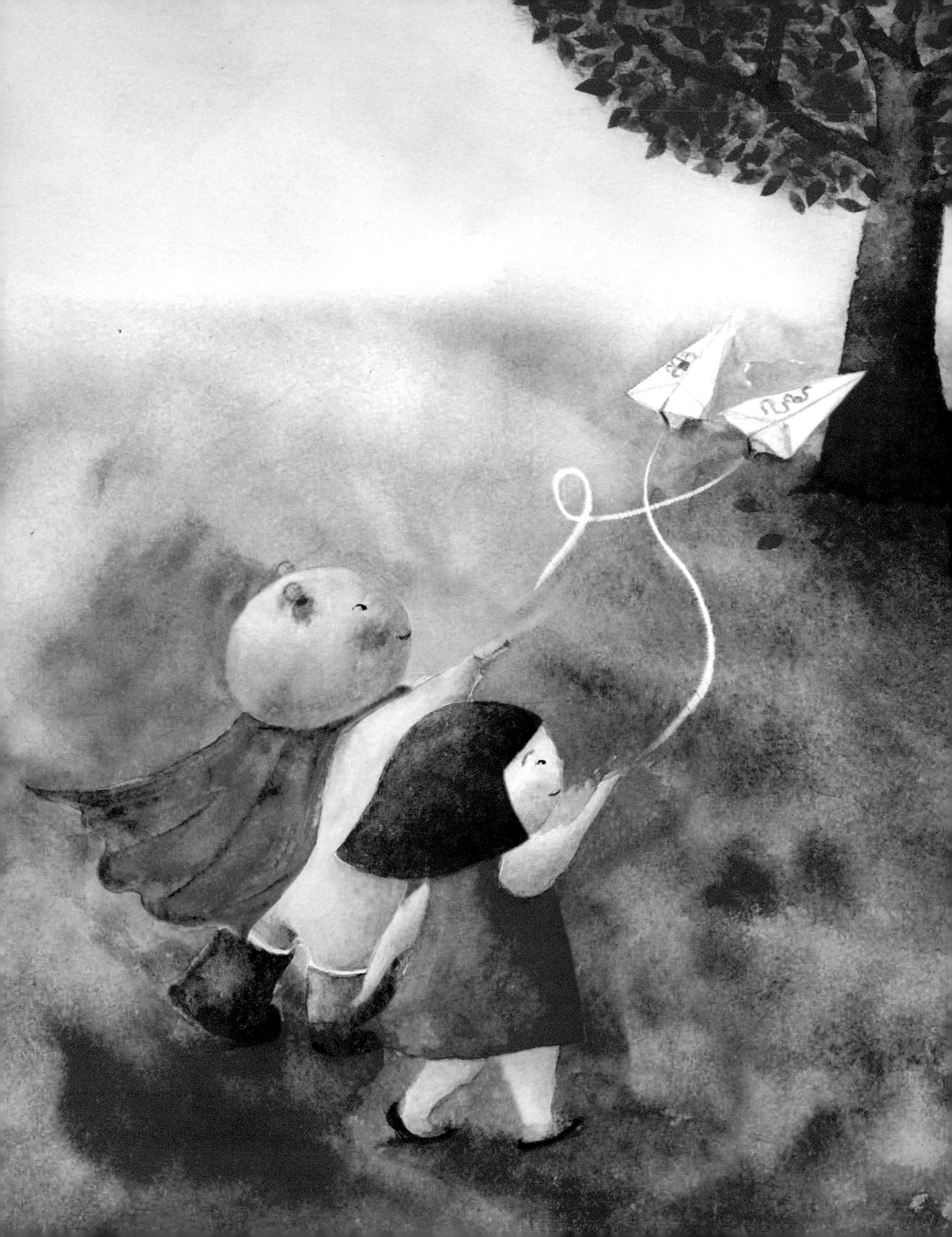

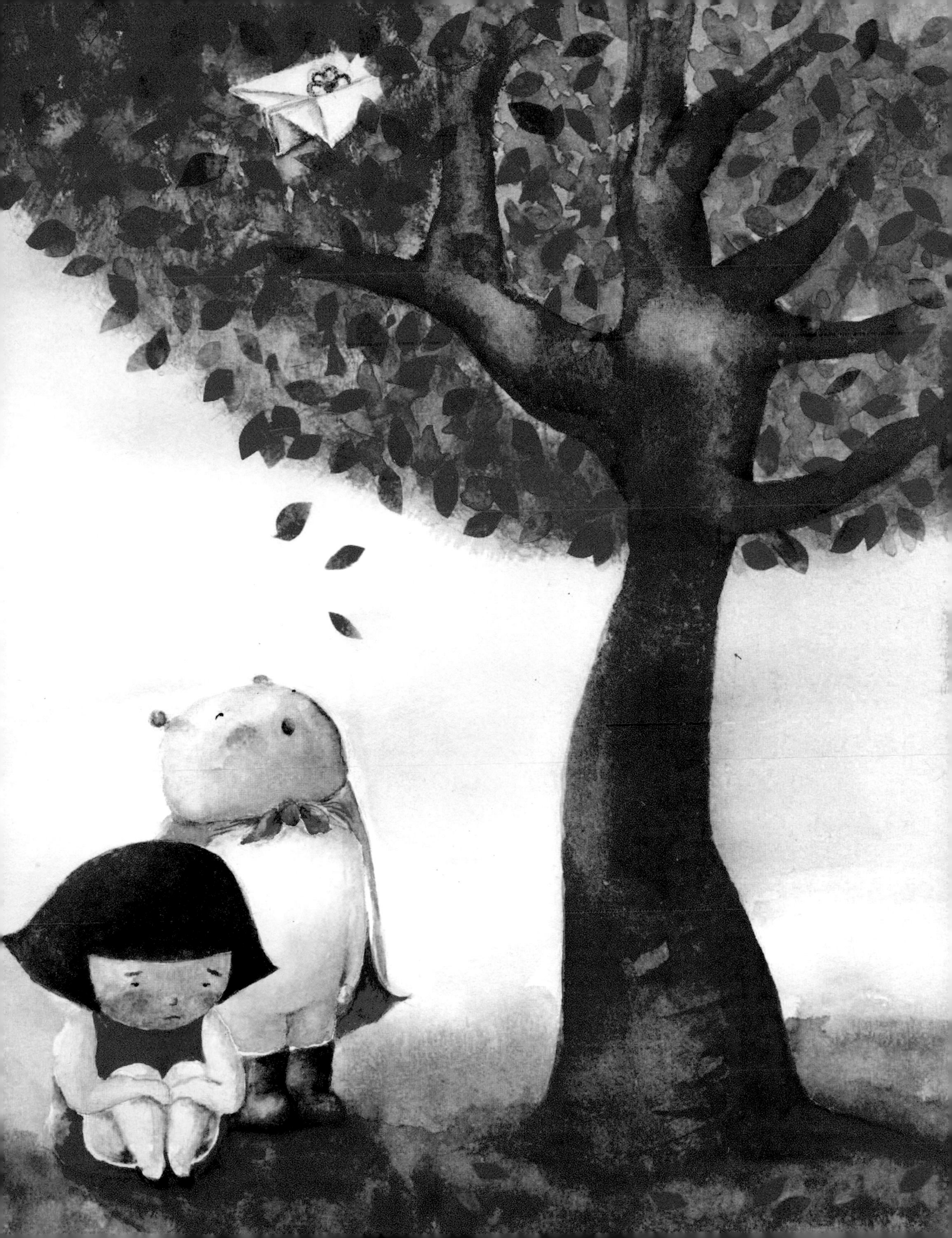

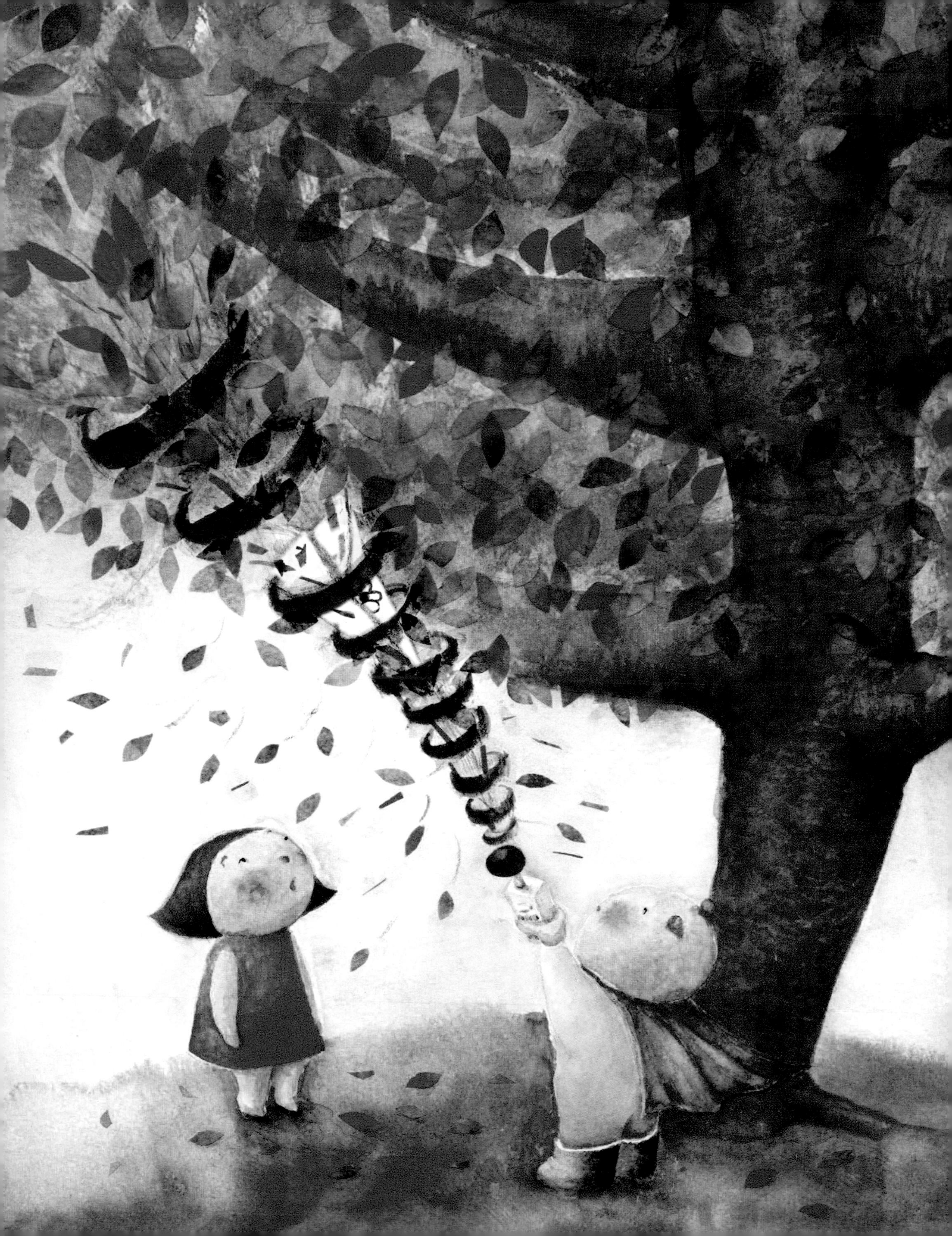

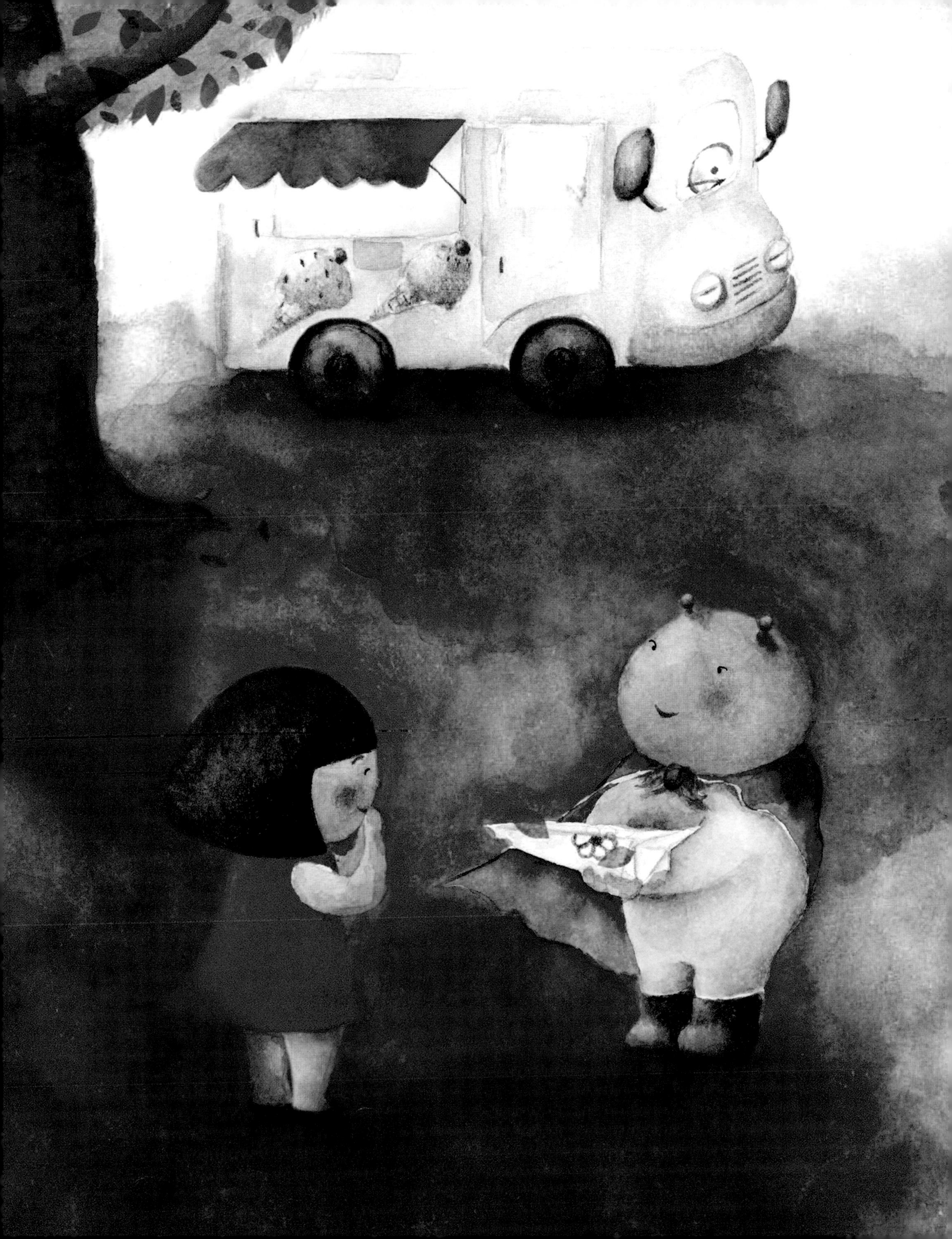

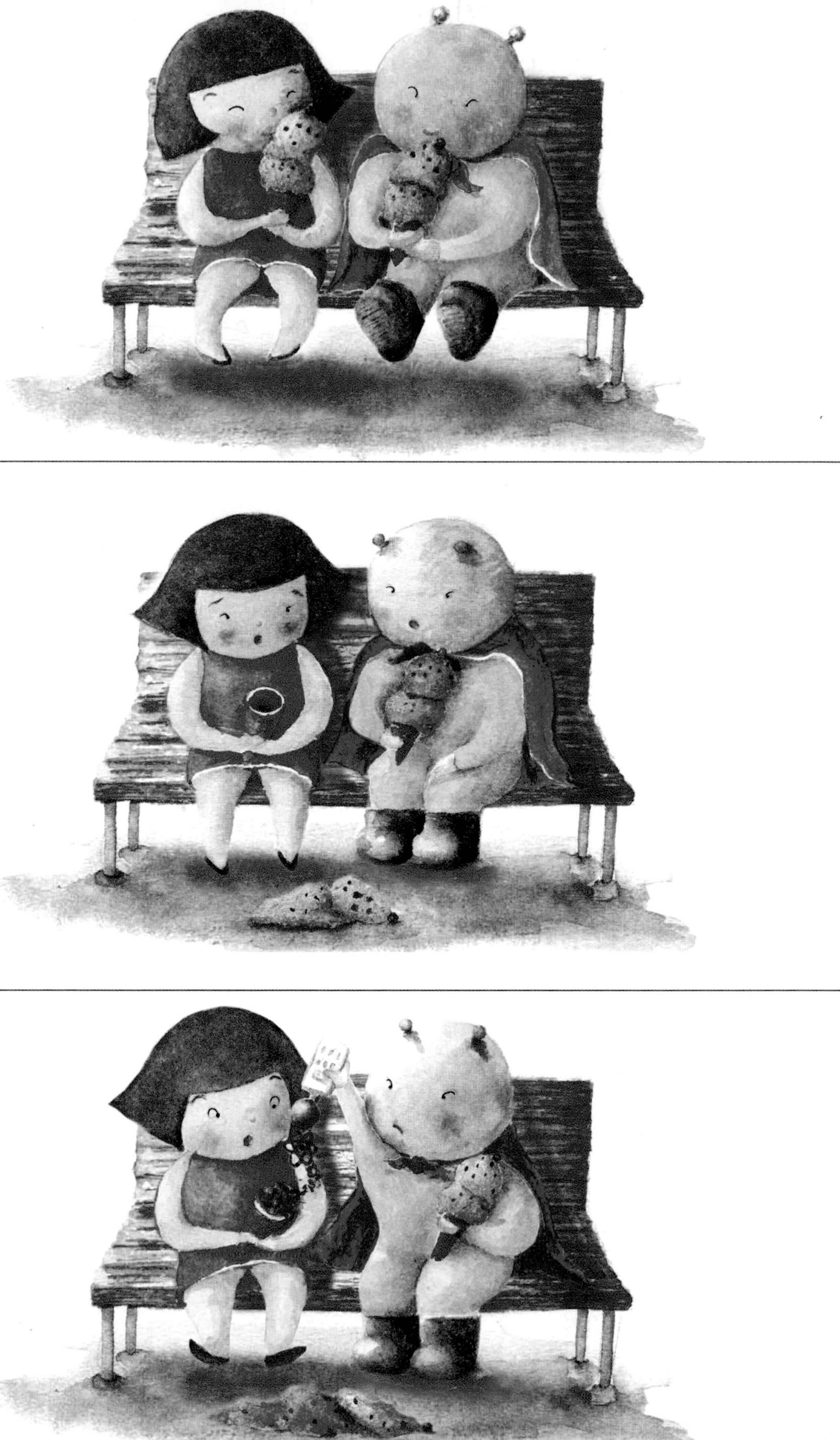

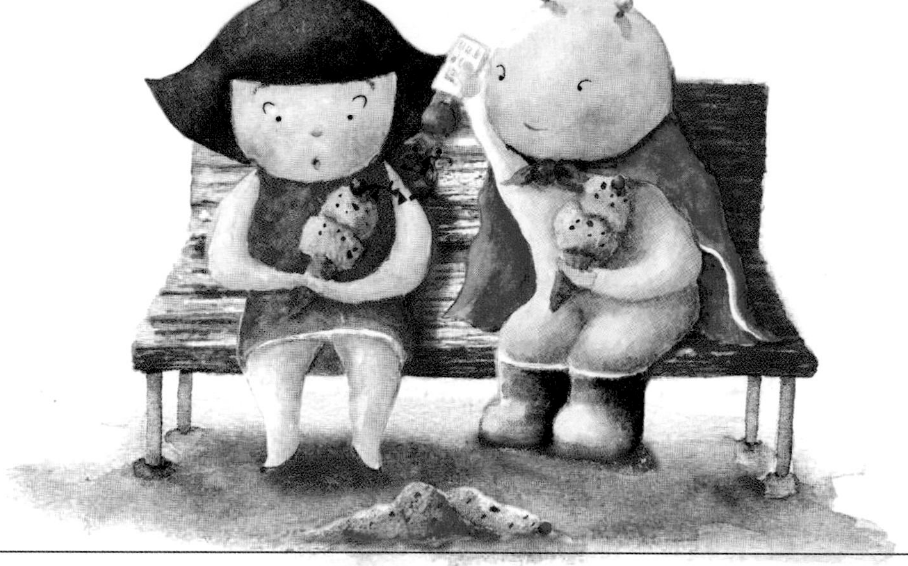
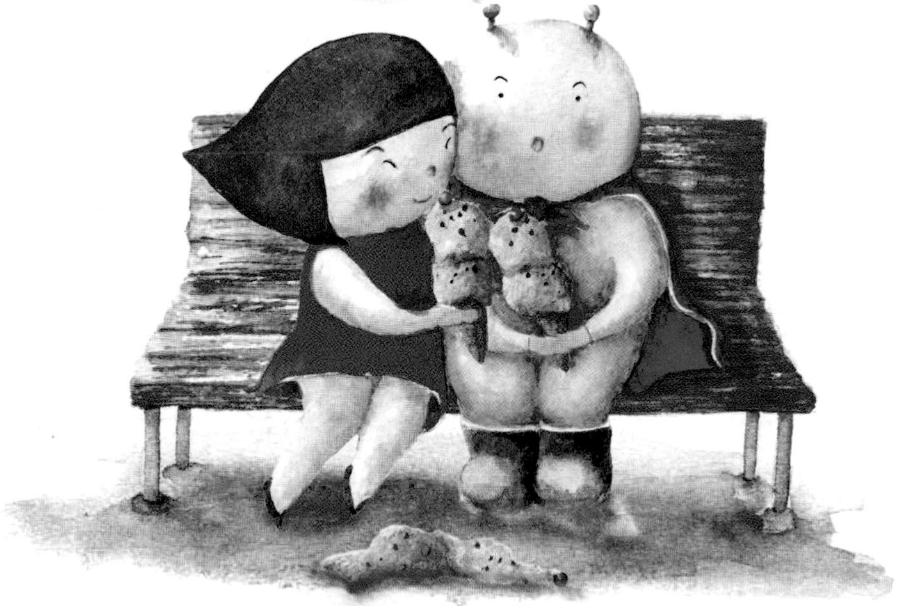
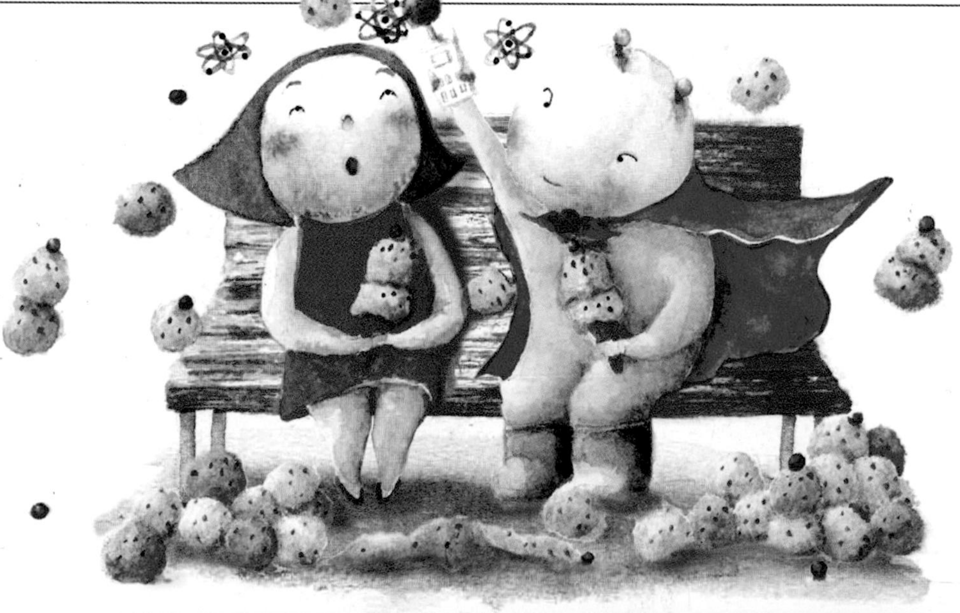

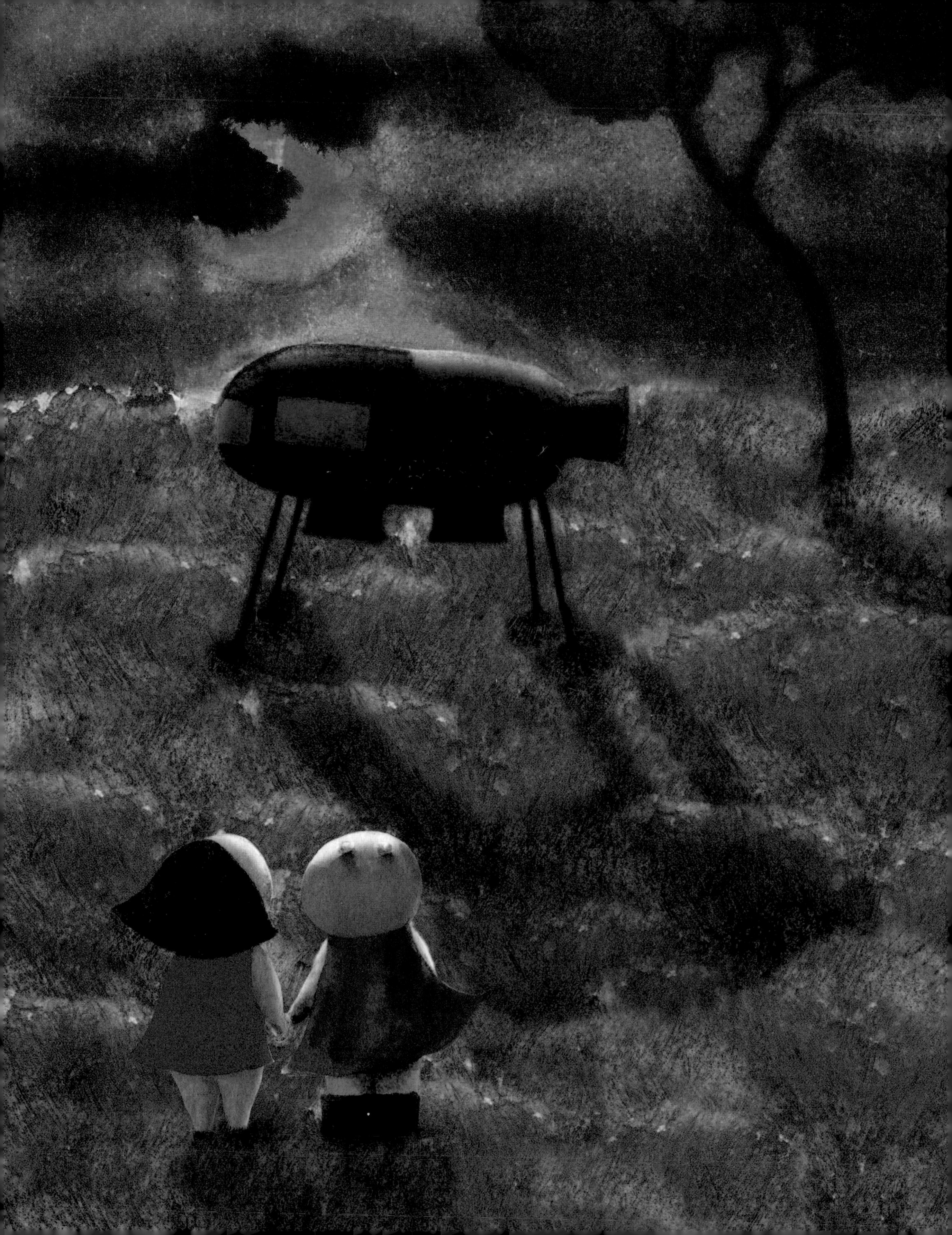

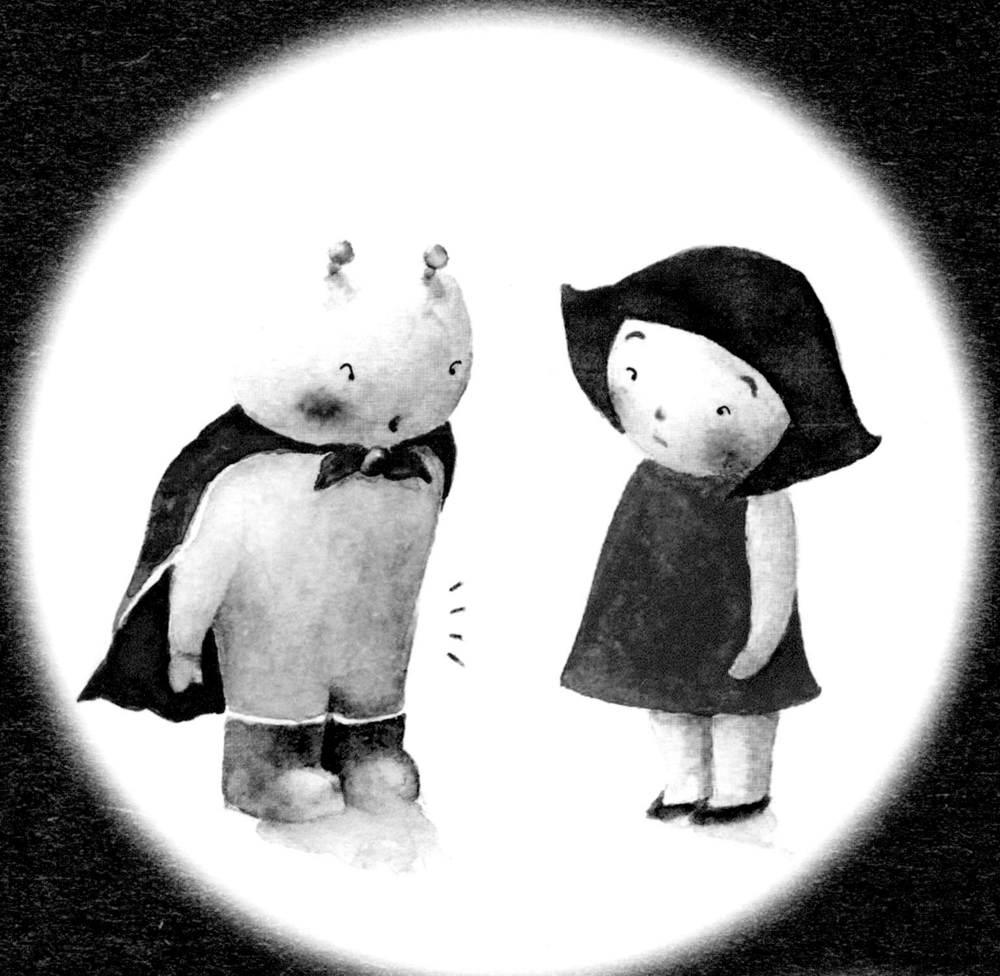

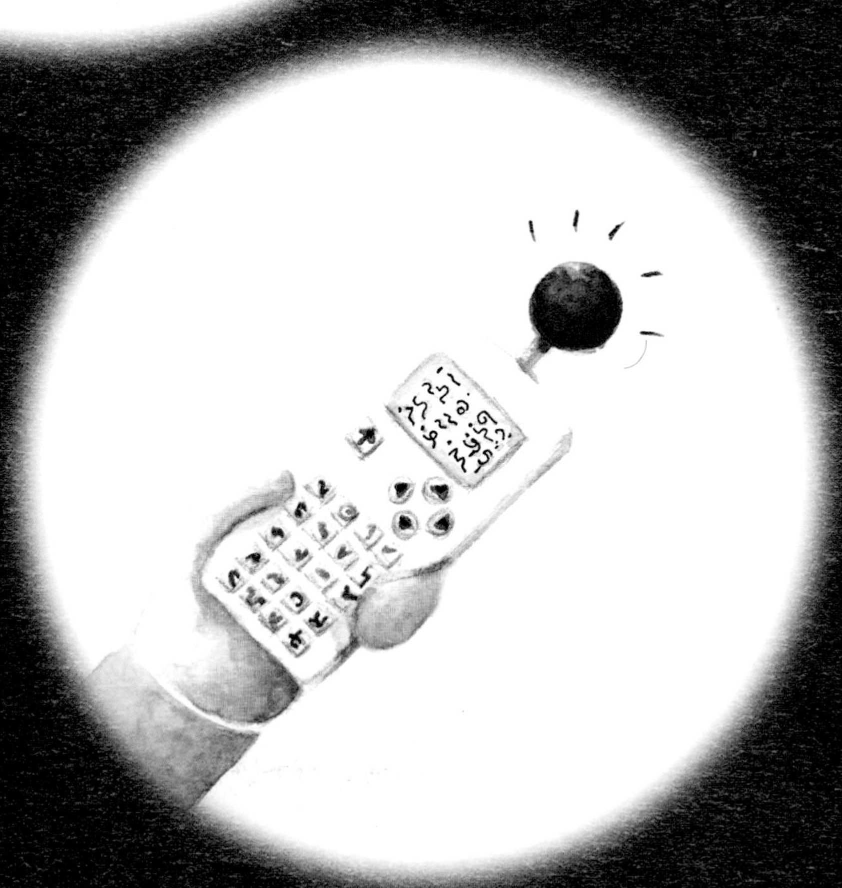

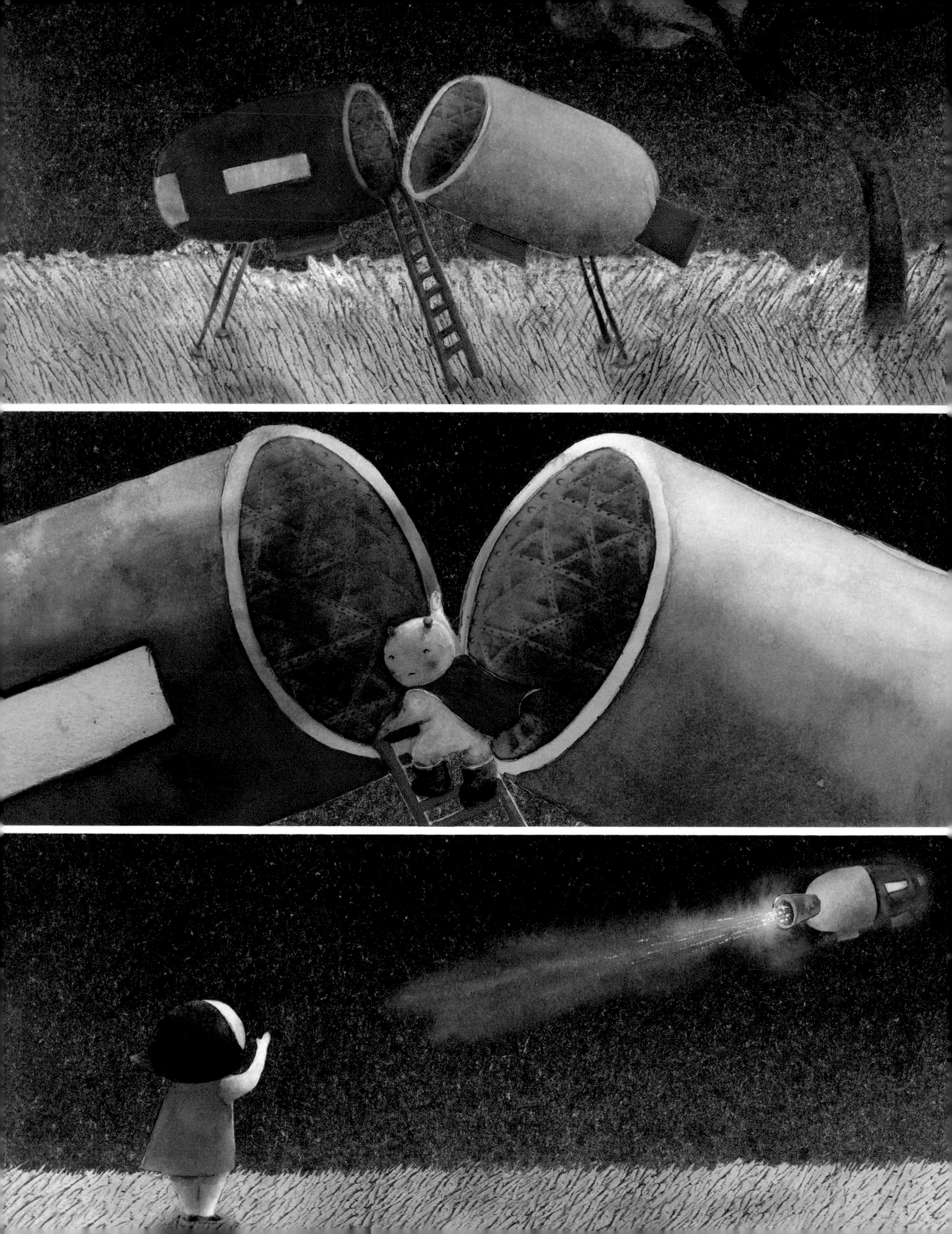

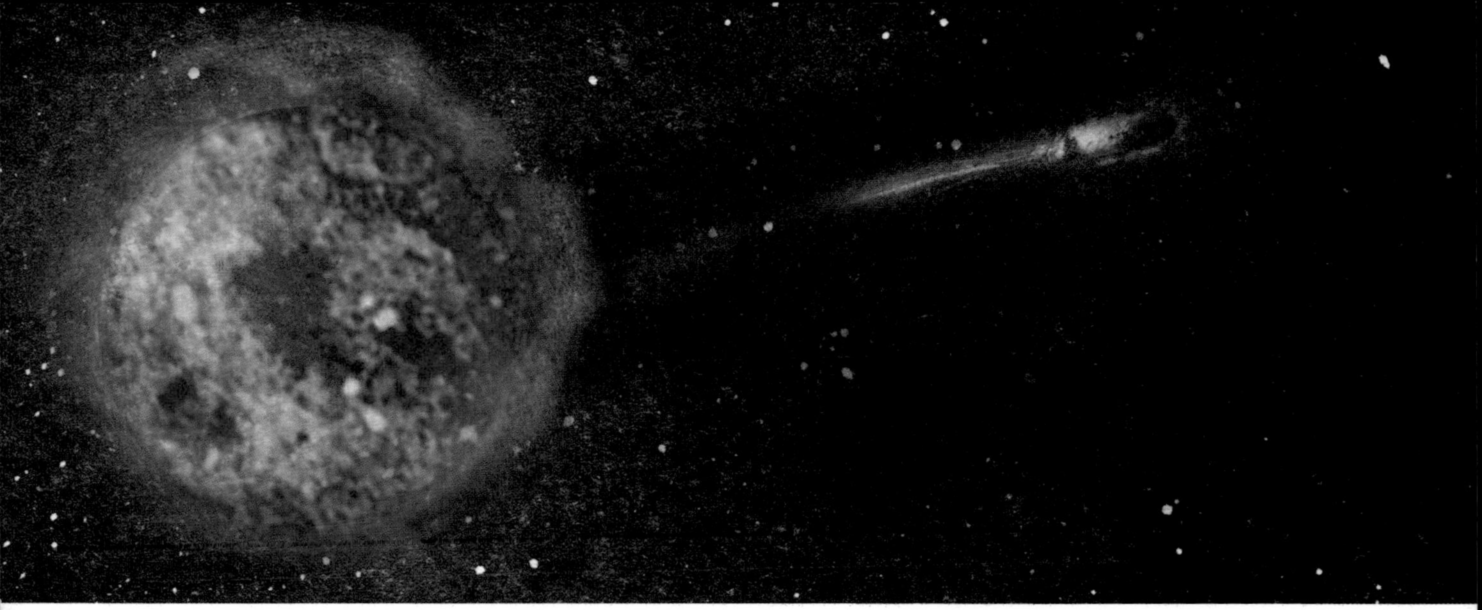

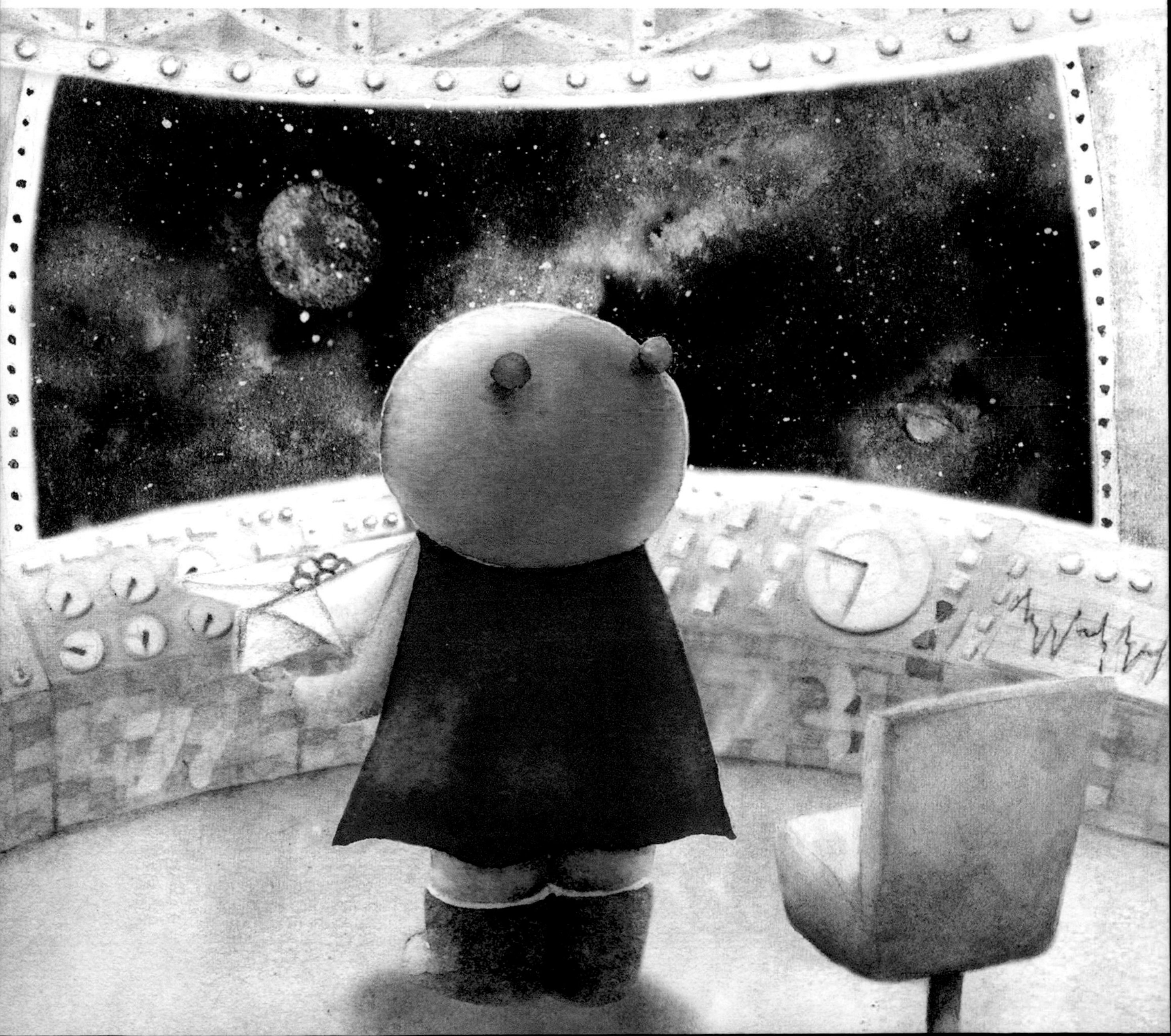

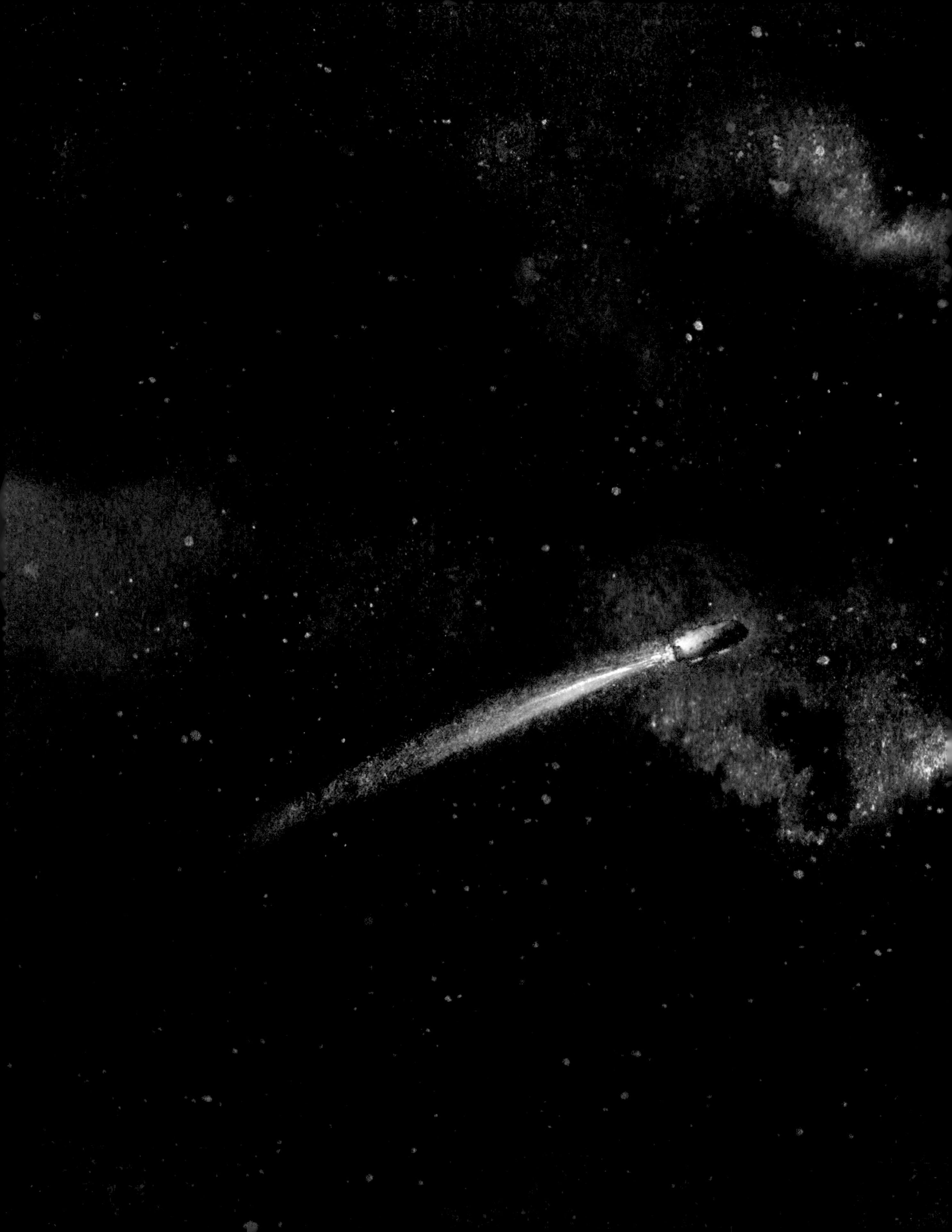

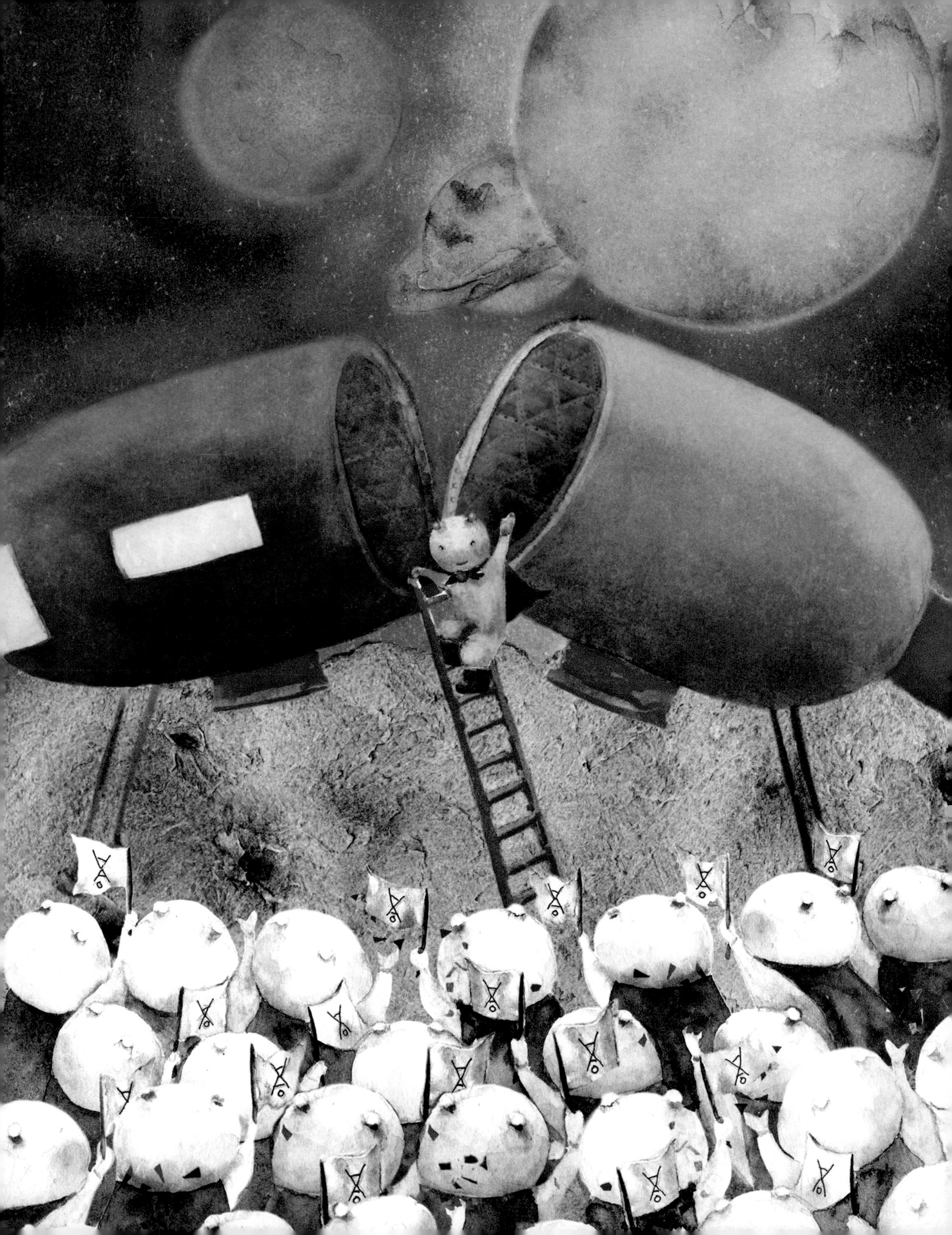

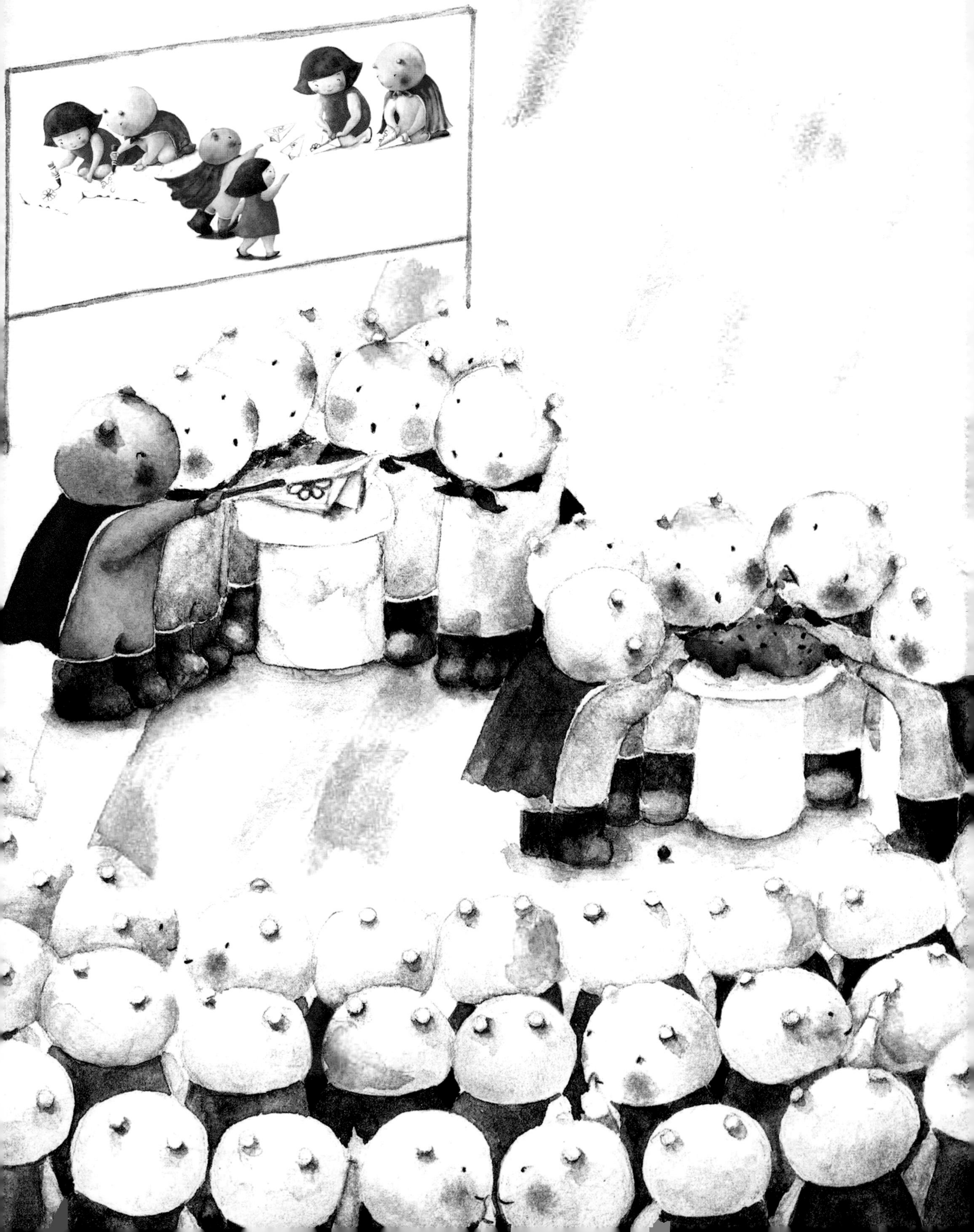

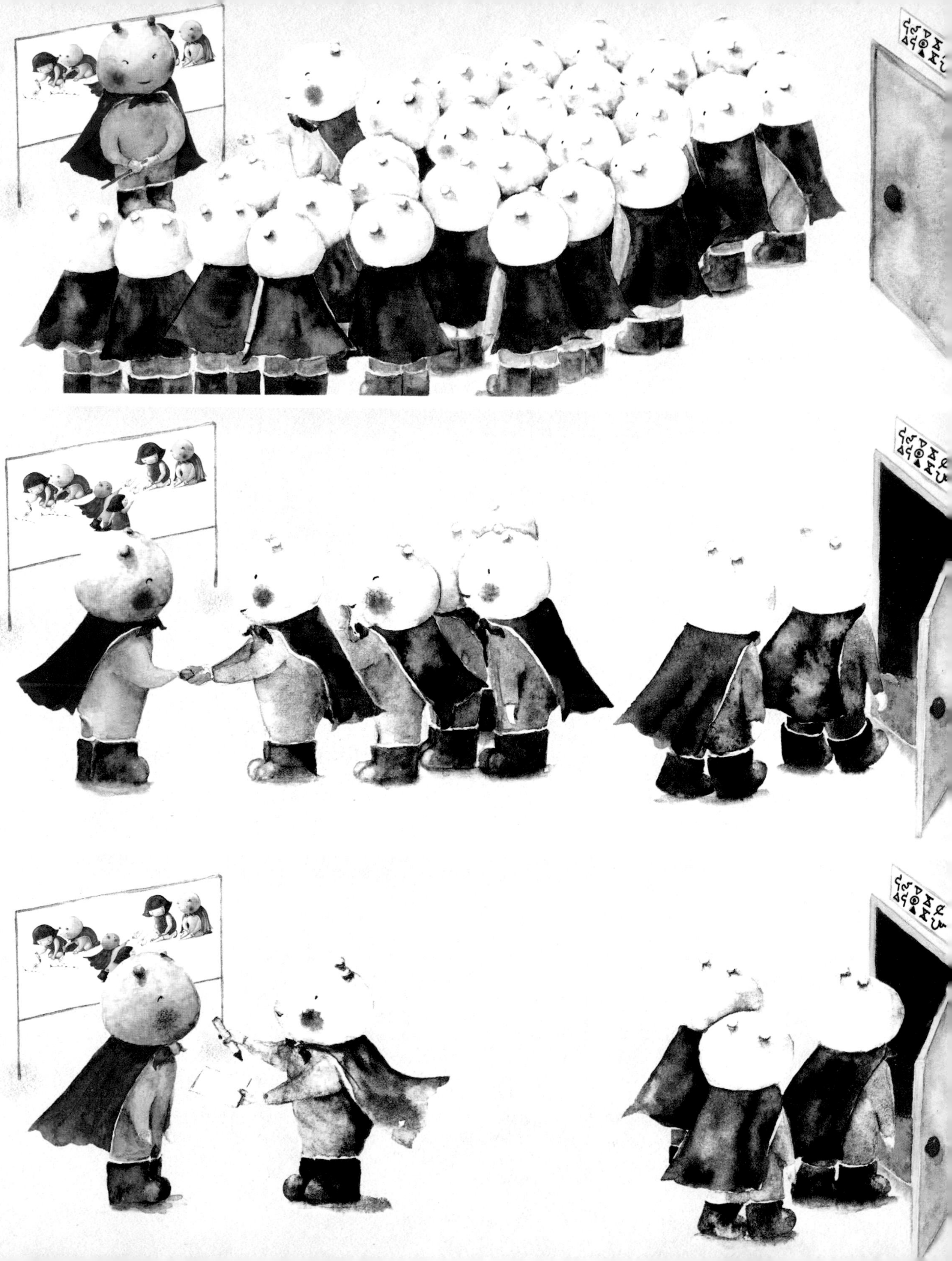

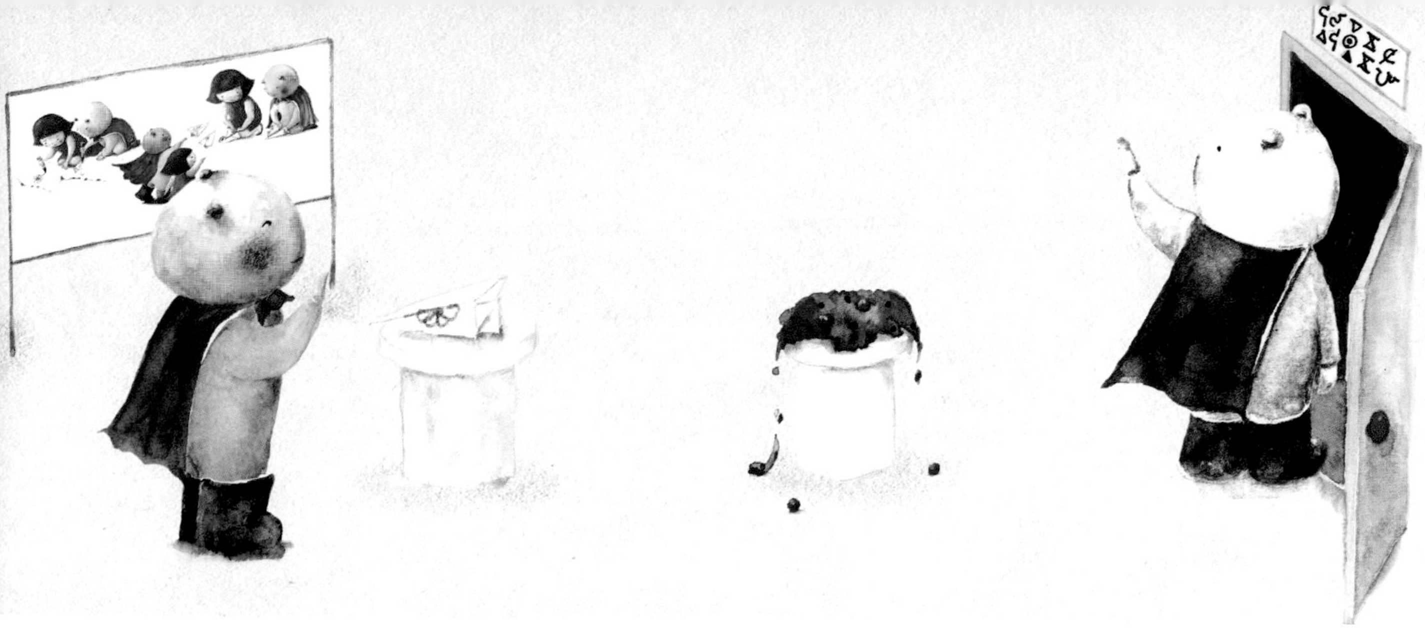

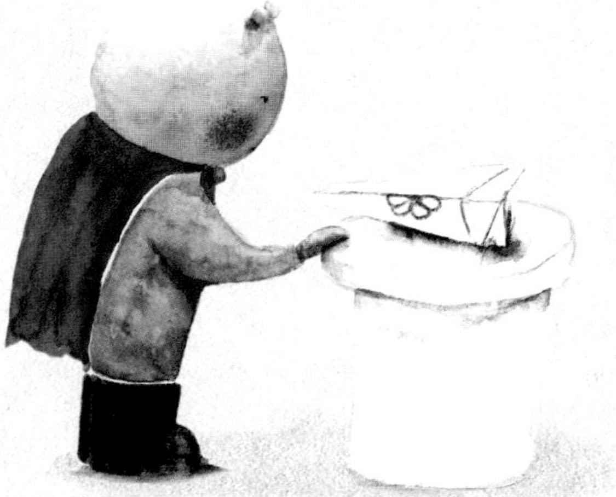

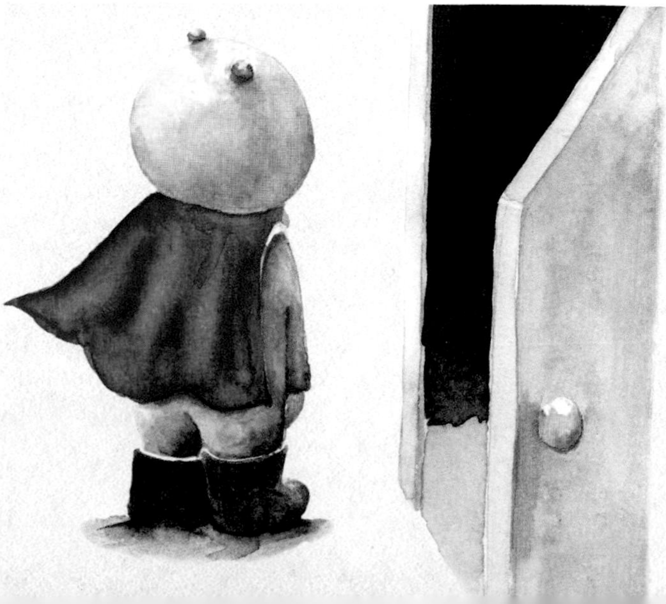

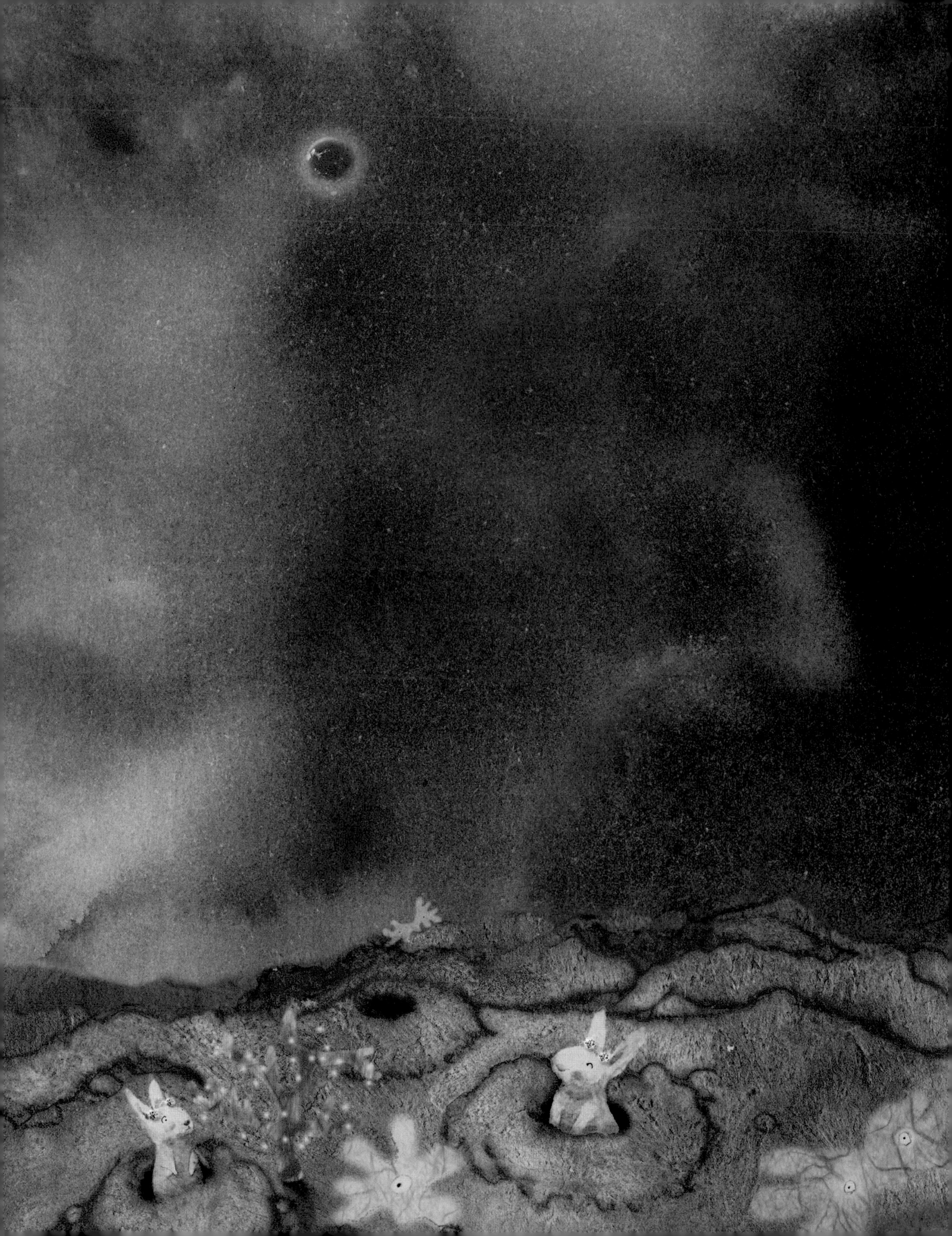

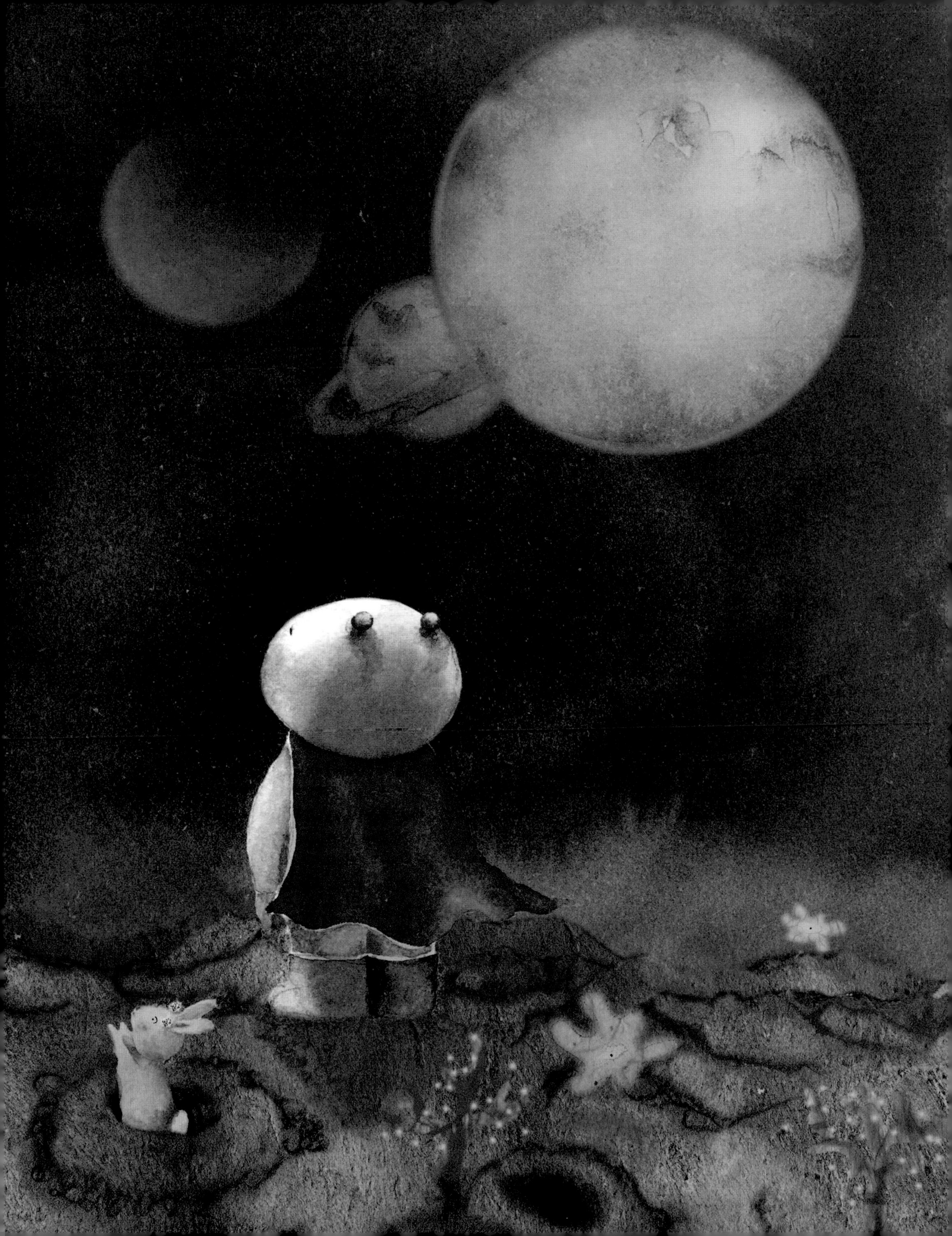

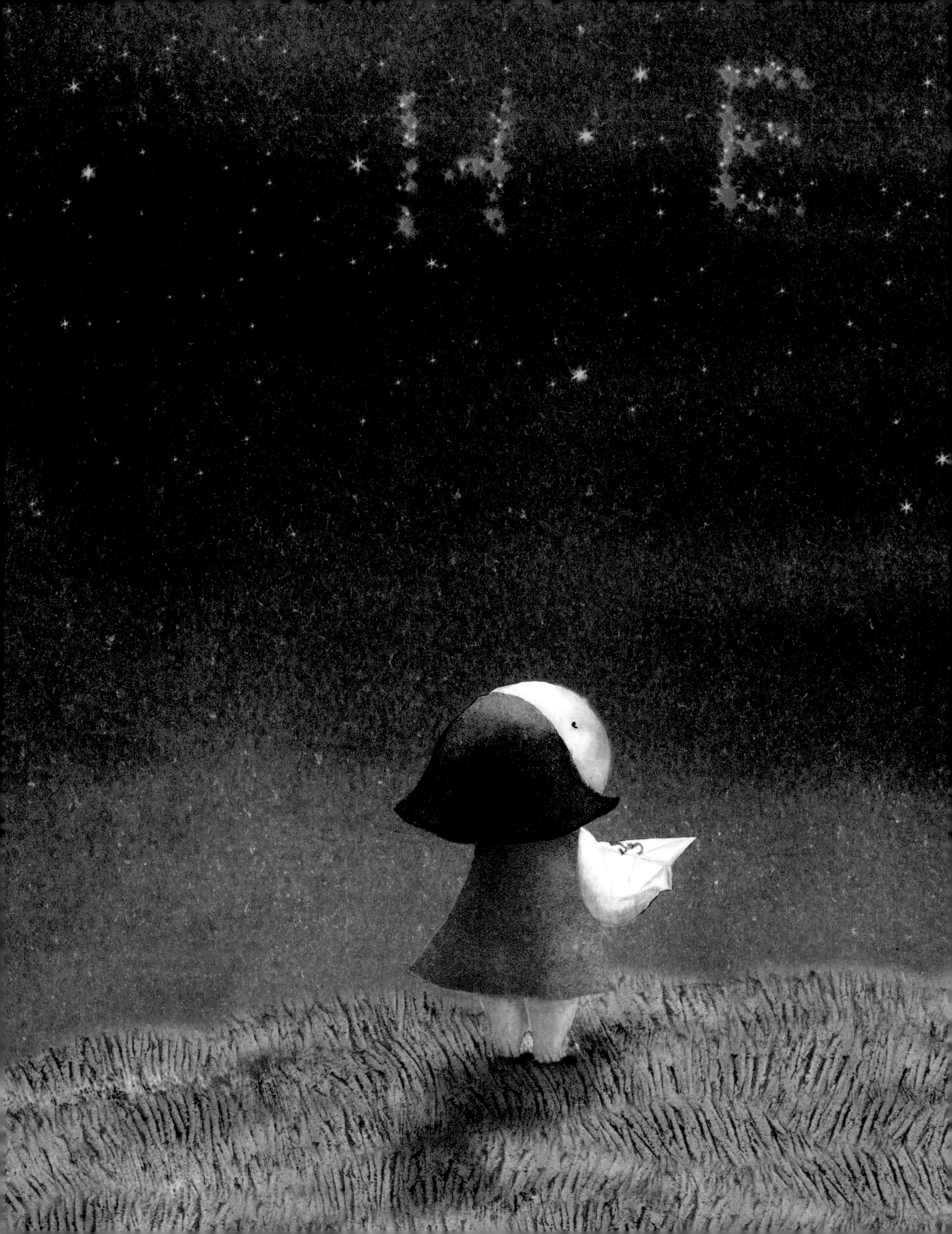